03/18

Prairie du Chien Memorial Library
125 S. Wacouta Ave
Prairie du Chien WI 53821
(608) 326-6211
Mon-Thu 9-8   Fri 9-5   Sat 9-1

JAKE MADDOX
GRAPHIC NOVELS

FACEOFF FALL OUT

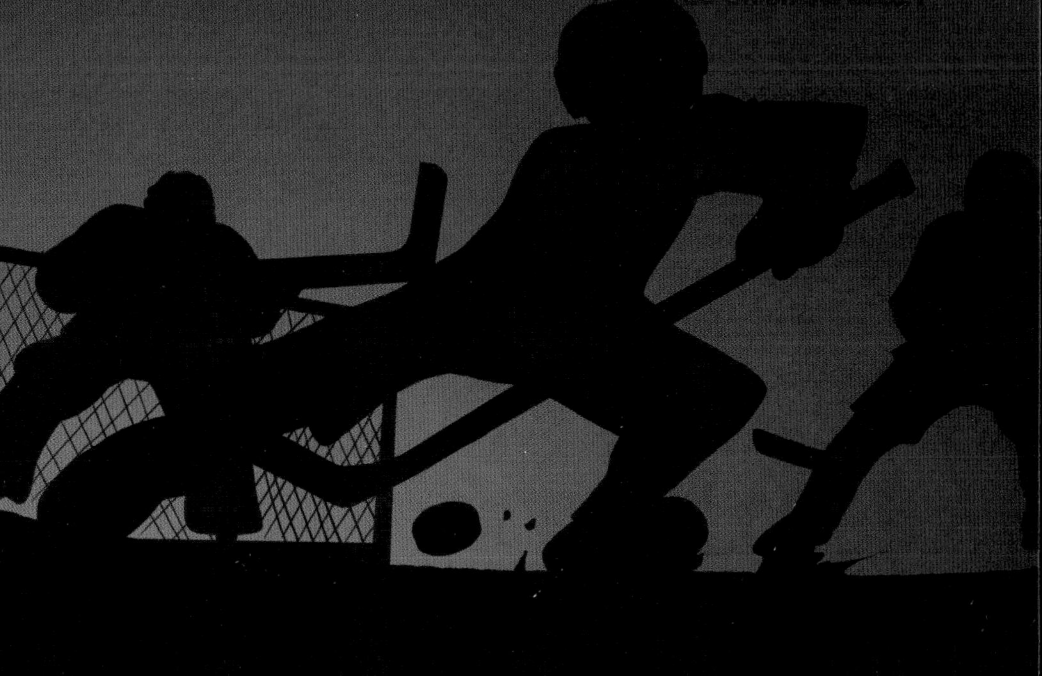

STONE ARCH BOOKS
a capstone imprint

JAKE MADDOX
GRAPHIC NOVELS

Jake Maddox Graphic Novels are published by
Stone Arch Books, a Capstone imprint
1710 Roe Crest Drive
North Mankato, Minnesota 56003

www.mycapstone.com

Library of Congress Cataloging-in-Publication Data
is available on the Library of Congress website.

ISBN: 978-1-4965-6043-8 (library binding)
ISBN: 978-1-4965-6047-6 (paperback)
ISBN: 978-1-4965-6051-3 (ebook PDF)

Summary: When Jackson "Jax" Kingsford gets to
play in the state hockey tournament, he has to play
against Archer Foss. The two were once neighbors,
teammates, and the best of friends. But then
Archer's family moved across town, splitting up
the team and their friendship. What will happen
when Jax and Archer face off against each other in
the big game?

Editor: Aaron J. Sautter
Designer: Brann Garvey
Production: Laura Manthe

Printed in the United States of America.
010836S18

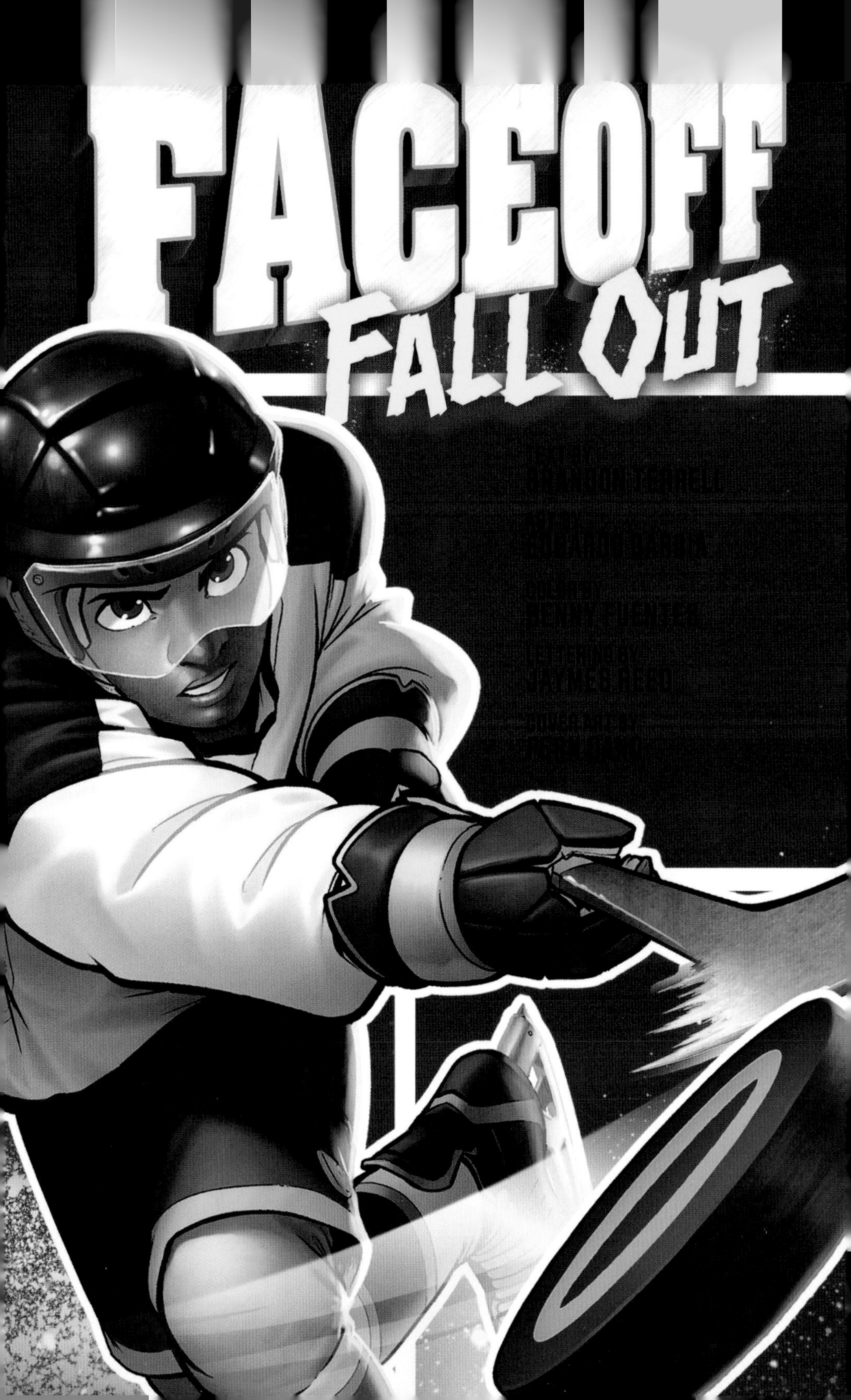
FACEOFF
FALL OUT

STARTING LINEUP

JACKSON (JAX) KINGSFORD

ARCHER FOSS

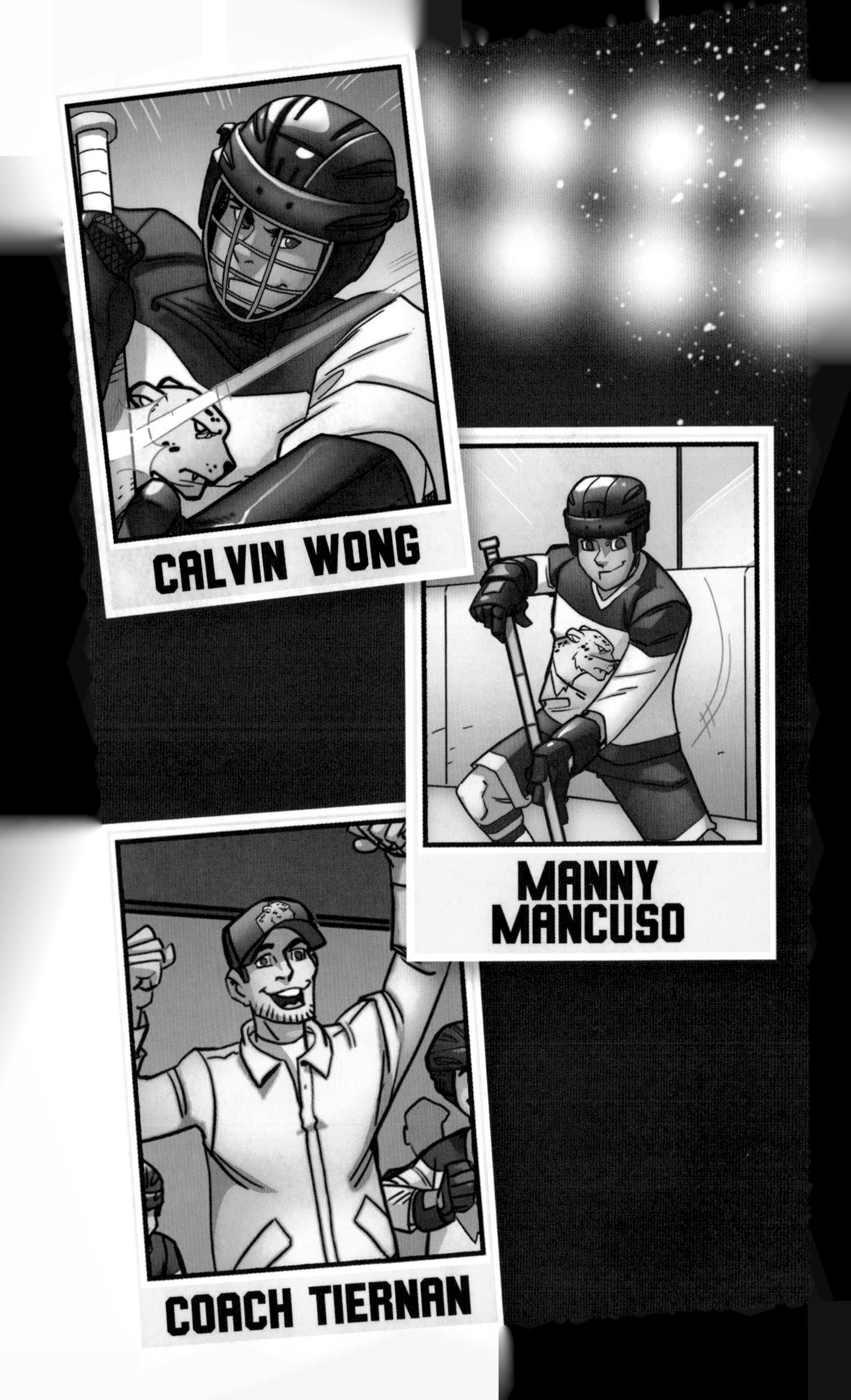
CALVIN WONG
MANNY MANCUSO
COACH TIERNAN

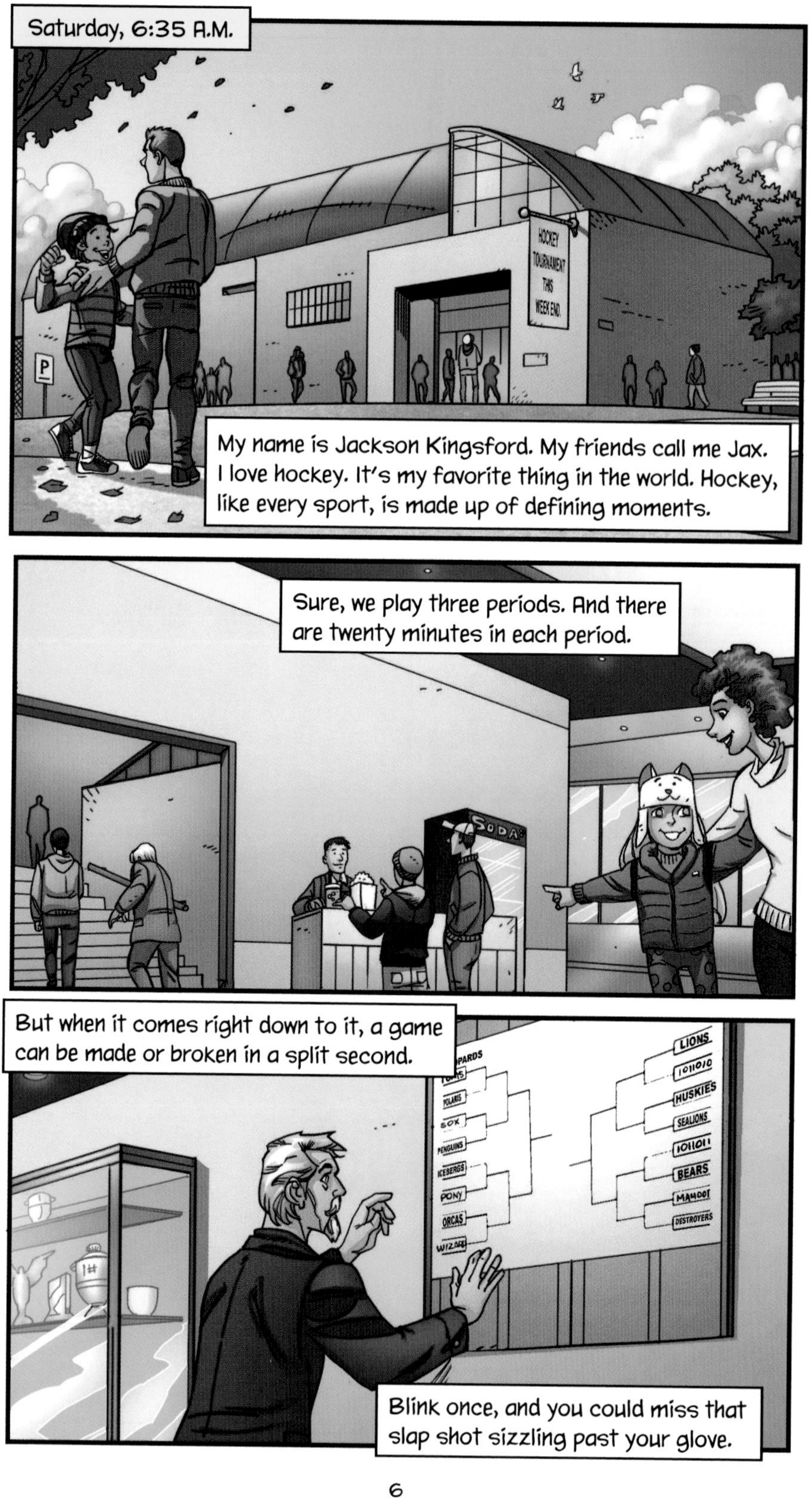
Saturday, 6:35 A.M.
HOCKEY TOURNAMENT THIS WEEK END.
P
My name is Jackson Kingsford. My friends call me Jax. I love hockey. It's my favorite thing in the world. Hockey, like every sport, is made up of defining moments.
Sure, we play three periods. And there are twenty minutes in each period.
SODA
But when it comes right down to it, a game can be made or broken in a split second.
POLARIS
SOX
PENGUINS
ICEBERGS
PONY
ORCAS
LIONS
HUSKIES
SEALIONS
BEARS
DESTROYERS
Blink once, and you could miss that slap shot sizzling past your glove.

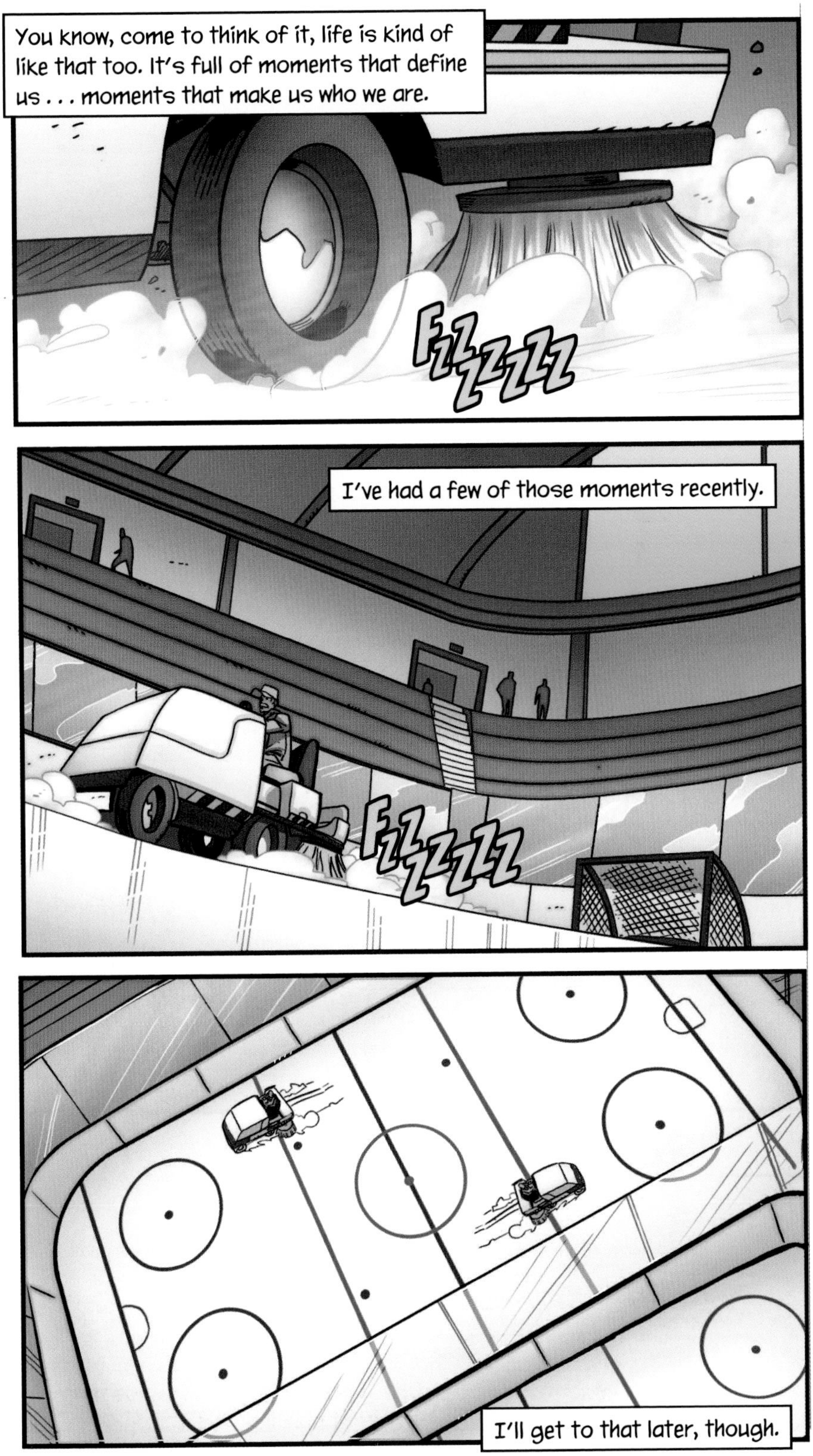
You know, come to think of it, life is kind of like that too. It's full of moments that define us . . . moments that make us who we are.
FZZZZZZ
I've had a few of those moments recently.
FZZZZZZ
I'll get to that later, though.

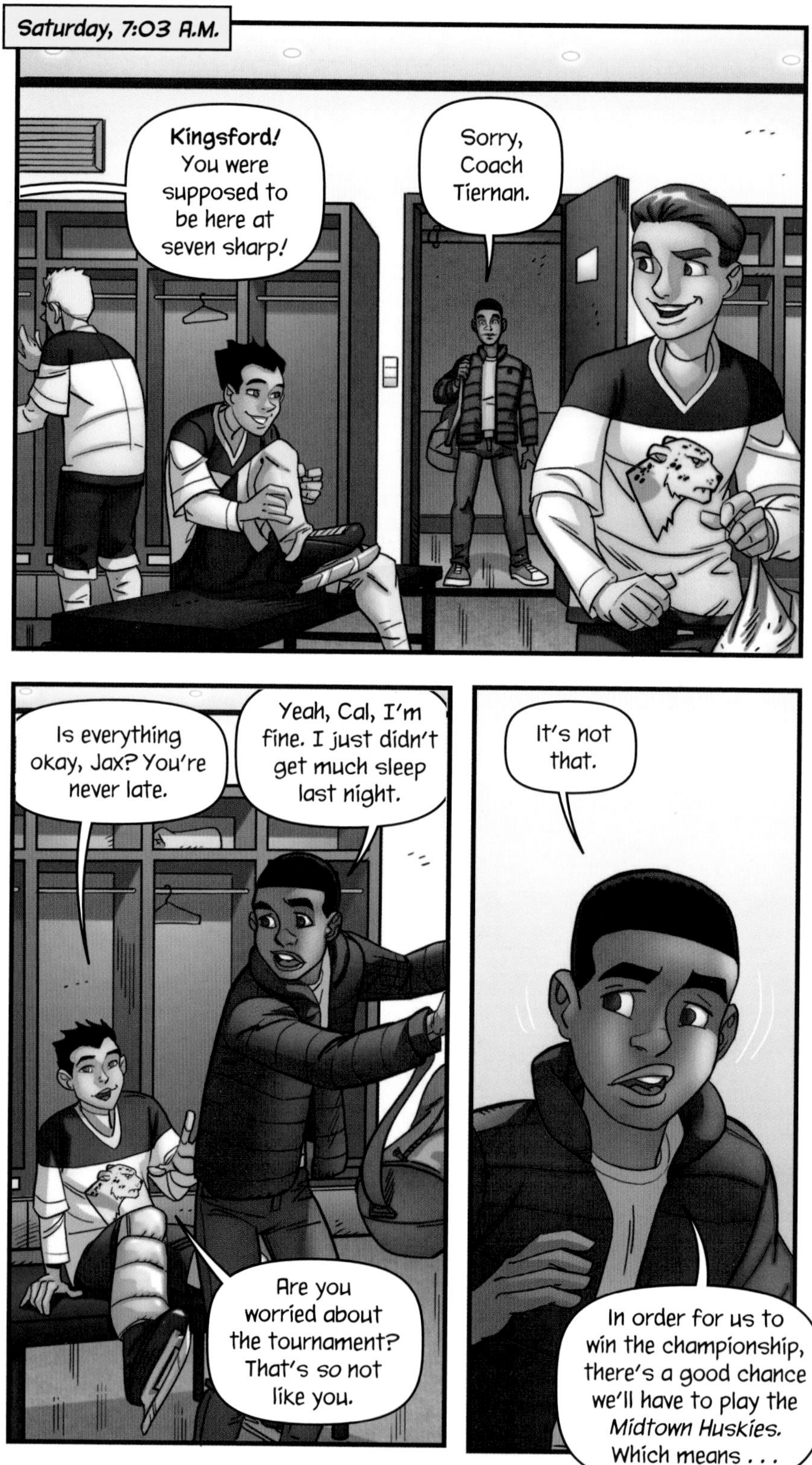
Saturday, 7:03 A.M.
Kingsford! You were supposed to be here at seven sharp!
Sorry, Coach Tiernan.
Is everything okay, Jax? You're never late.
Yeah, Cal, I'm fine. I just didn't get much sleep last night.
Are you worried about the tournament? That's so not like you.
It's not that.
In order for us to win the championship, there's a good chance we'll have to play the *Midtown Huskies.* Which means . . .

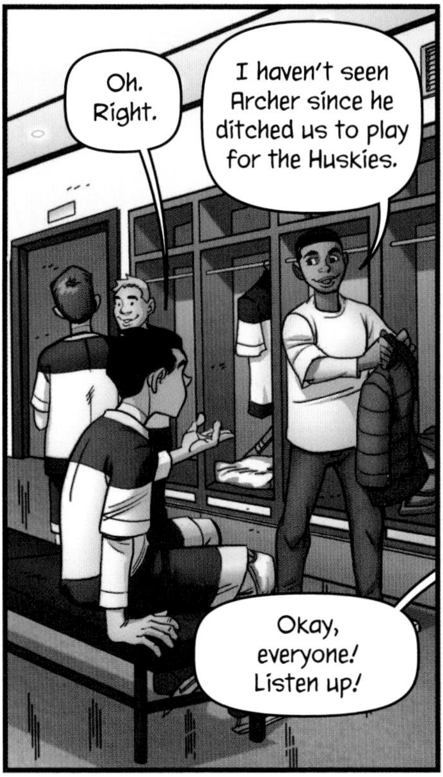
I haven't seen Archer since he ditched us to play for the Huskies.
Oh. Right.
Okay, everyone! Listen up!

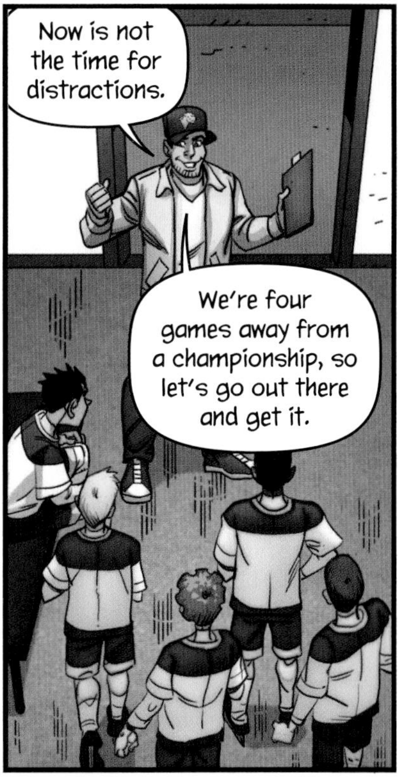
Now is not the time for distractions.
We're four games away from a championship, so let's go out there and get it.

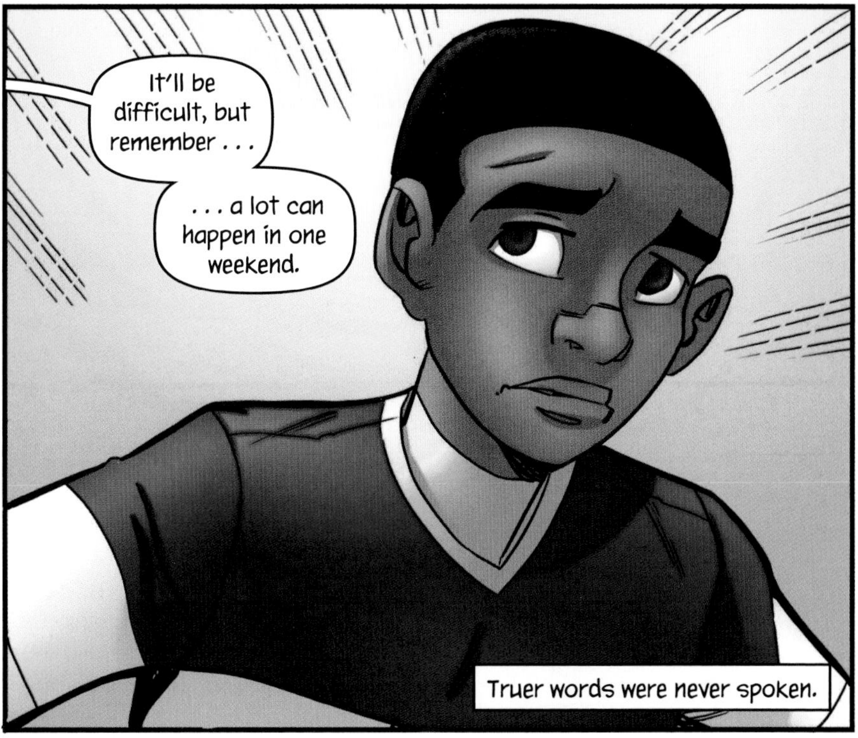
It'll be difficult, but remember . . .
. . . a lot can happen in one weekend.
Truer words were never spoken.

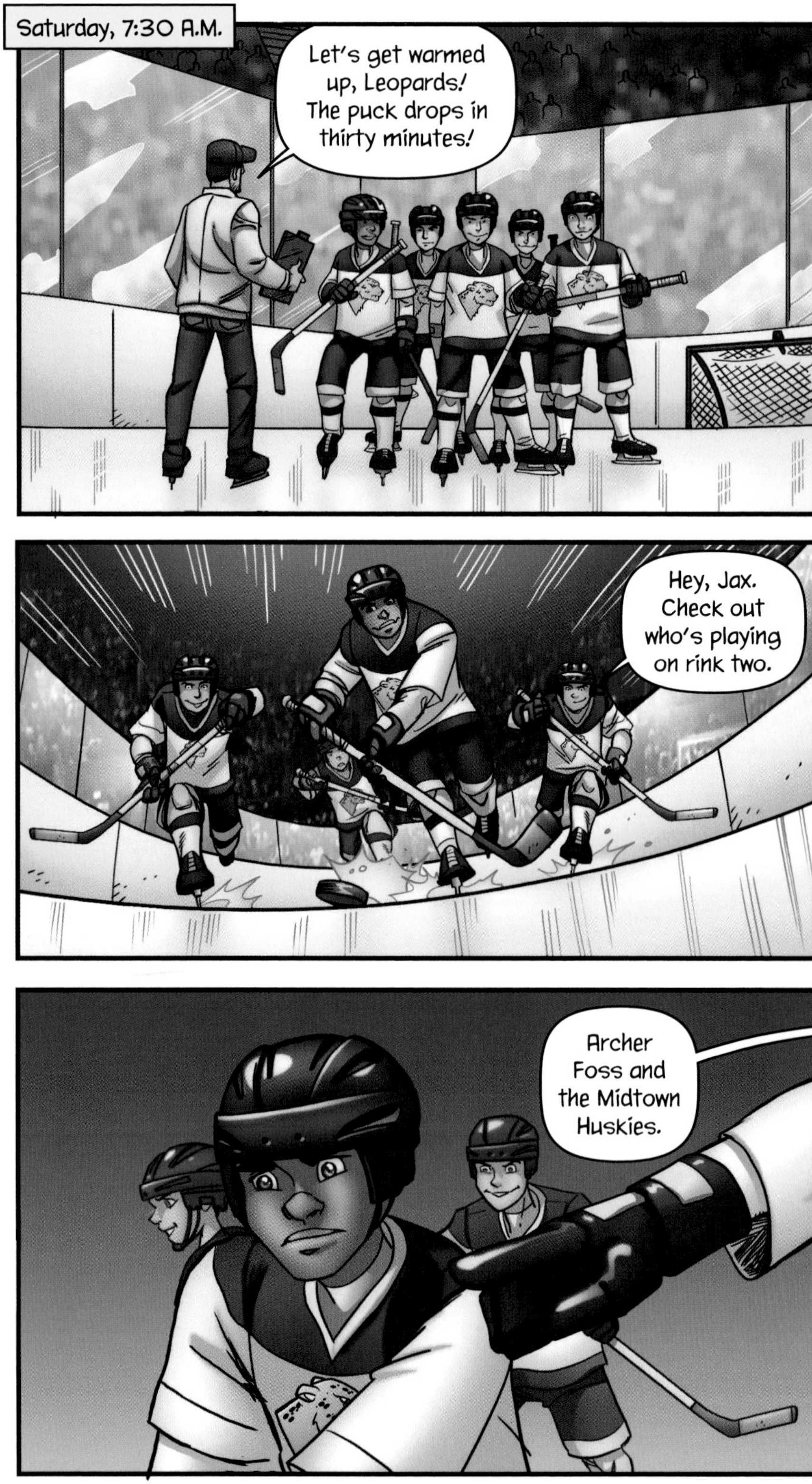
Saturday, 7:30 A.M.
Let's get warmed up, Leopards! The puck drops in thirty minutes!
Hey, Jax. Check out who's playing on rink two.
Archer Foss and the Midtown Huskies.

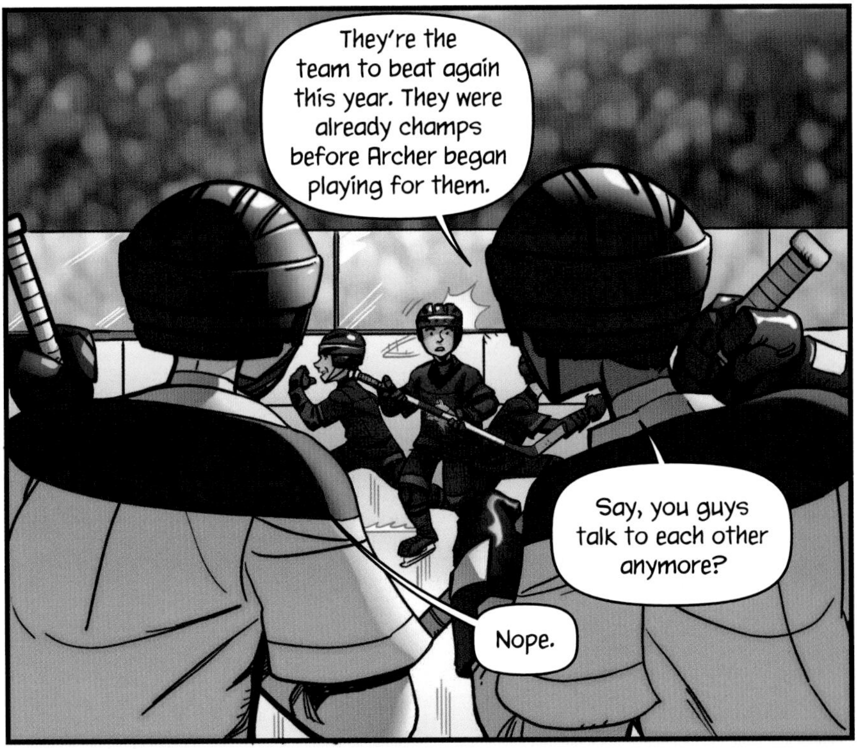
They're the team to beat again this year. They were already champs before Archer began playing for them.
Say, you guys talk to each other anymore?
Nope.

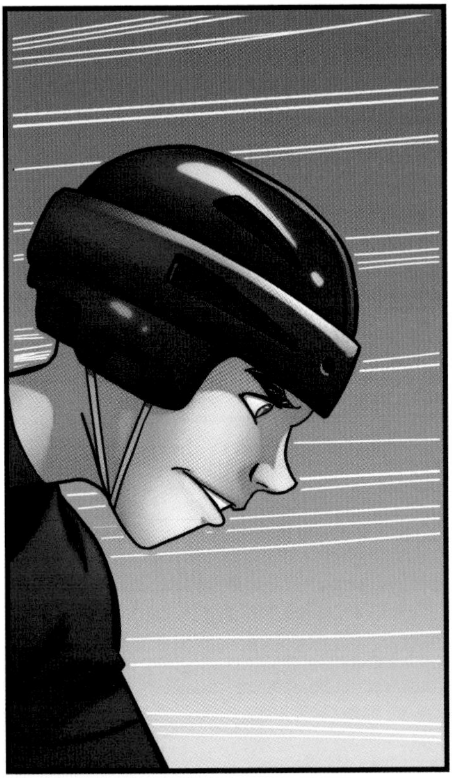

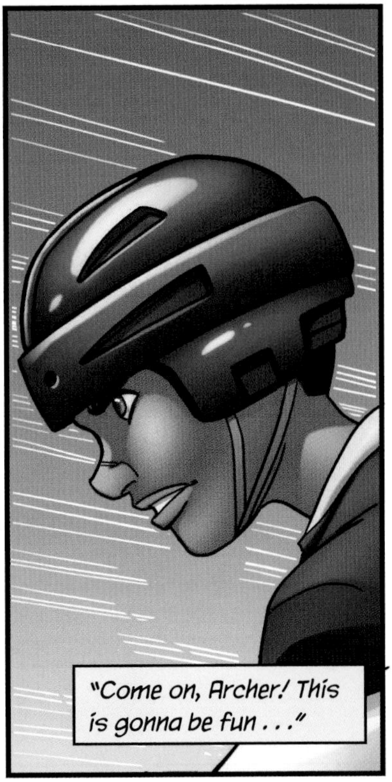
"Come on, Archer! This is gonna be fun . . ."

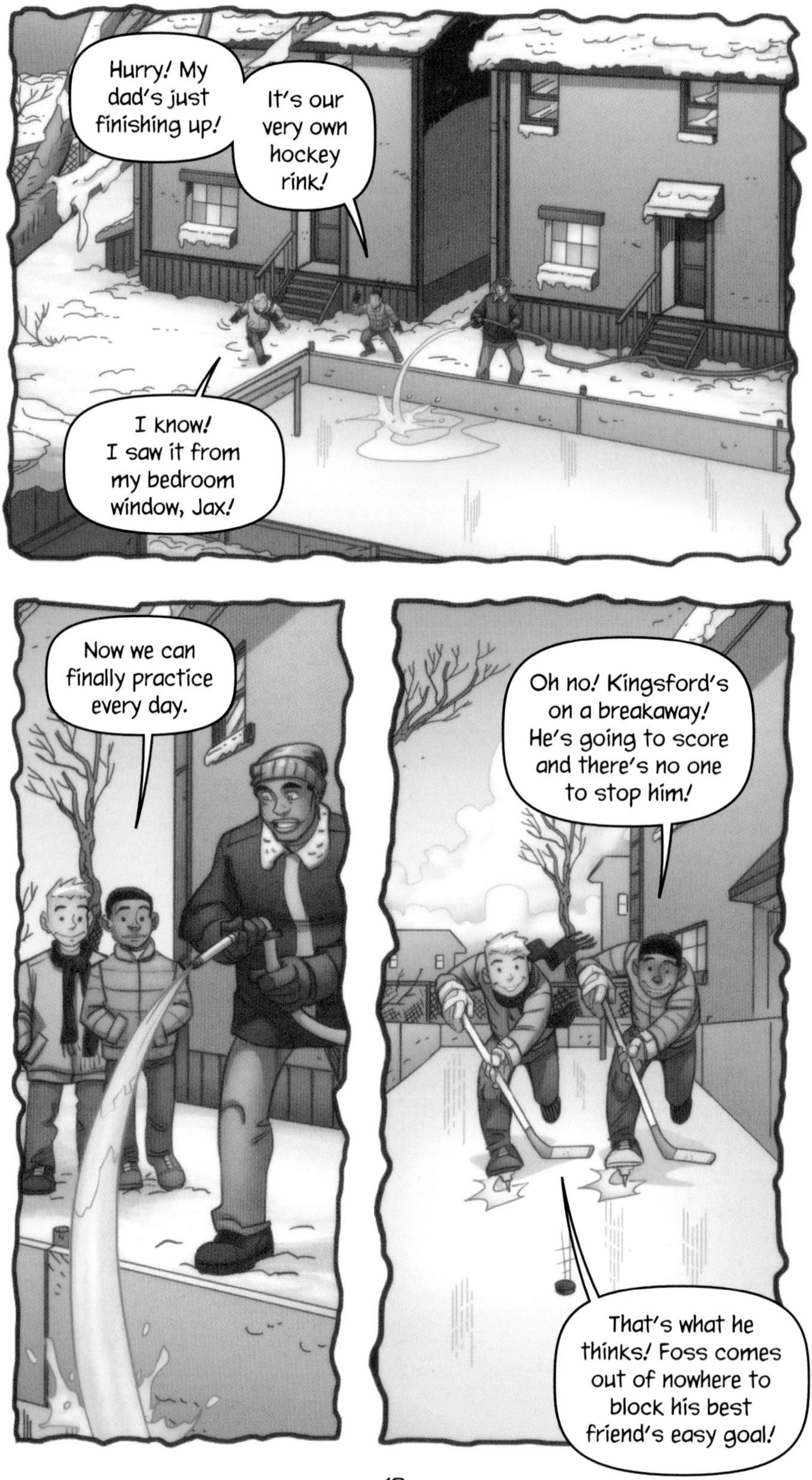
Hurry! My dad's just finishing up!
It's our very own hockey rink!
I know! I saw it from my bedroom window, Jax!
Now we can finally practice every day.
Oh no! Kingsford's on a breakaway! He's going to score and there's no one to stop him!
That's what he thinks! Foss comes out of nowhere to block his best friend's easy goal!

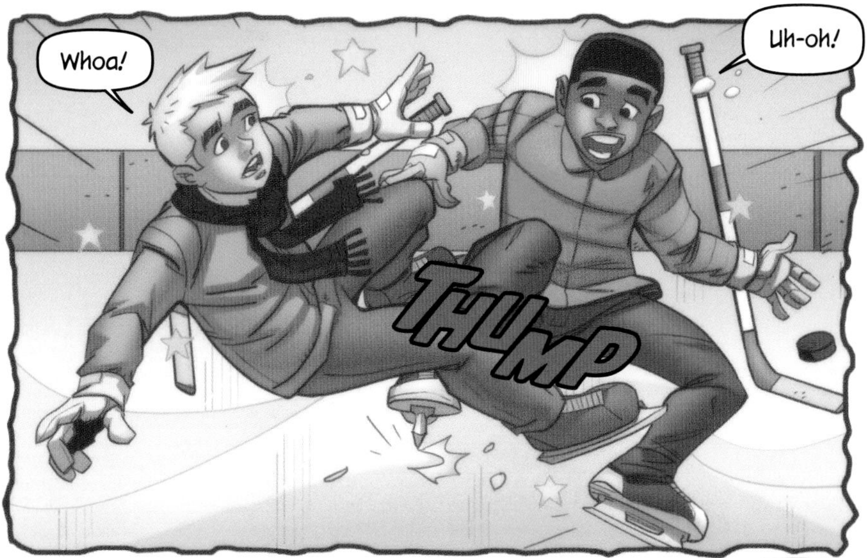
Whoa!
Uh-oh!
THUMP

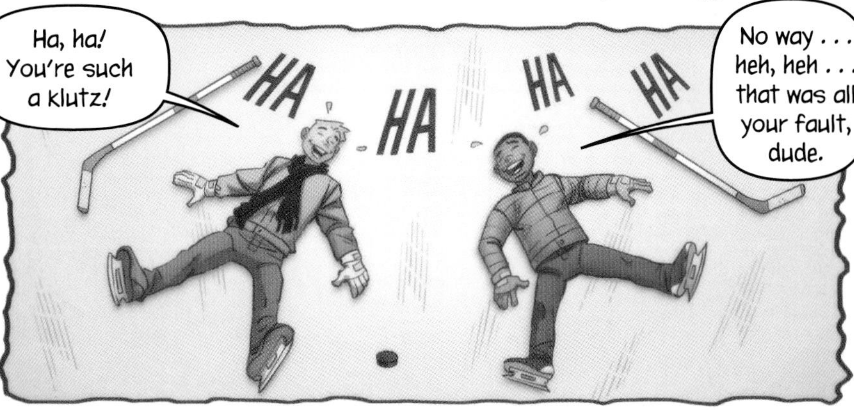
Ha, ha! You're such a klutz!
HA
HA
HA
HA
No way . . . heh, heh . . . that was all your fault, dude.

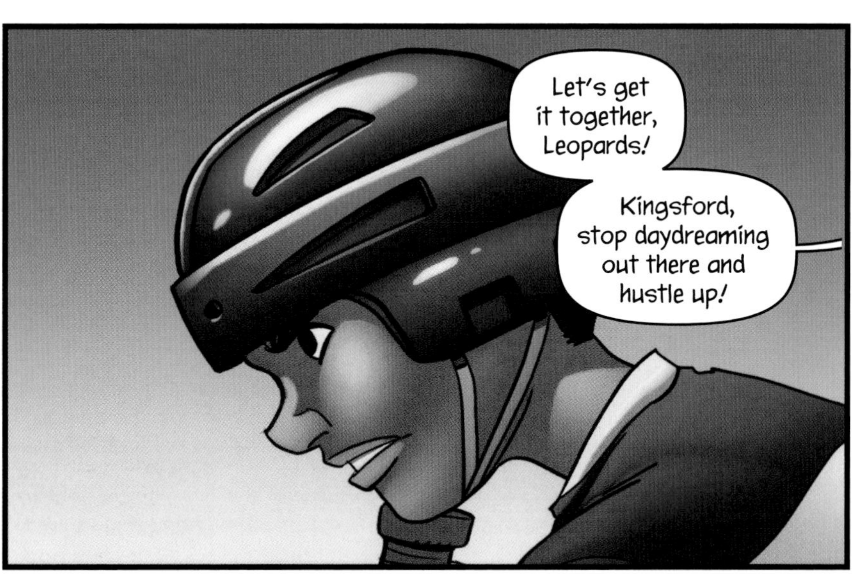
Let's get it together, Leopards!
Kingsford, stop daydreaming out there and hustle up!

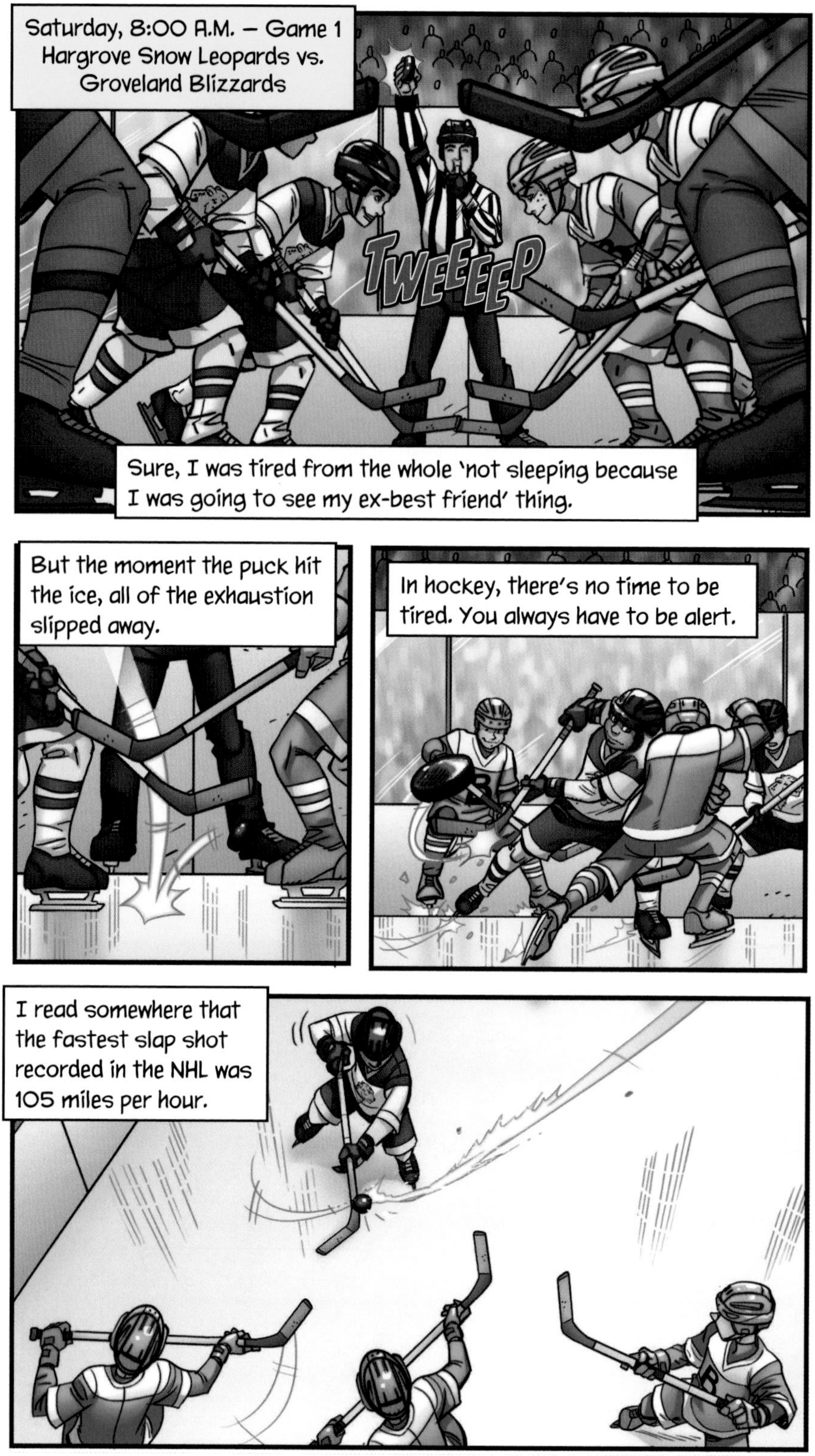
Saturday, 8:00 A.M. — Game 1
Hargrove Snow Leopards vs.
Groveland Blizzards
TWEEEEEP
Sure, I was tired from the whole 'not sleeping because I was going to see my ex-best friend' thing.
But the moment the puck hit the ice, all of the exhaustion slipped away.
In hockey, there's no time to be tired. You always have to be alert.
I read somewhere that the fastest slap shot recorded in the NHL was 105 miles per hour.

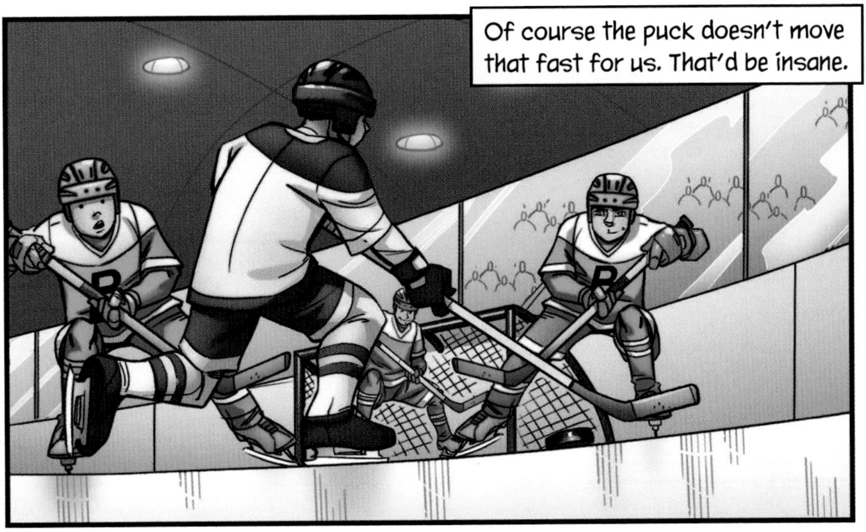
Of course the puck doesn't move that fast for us. That'd be insane.

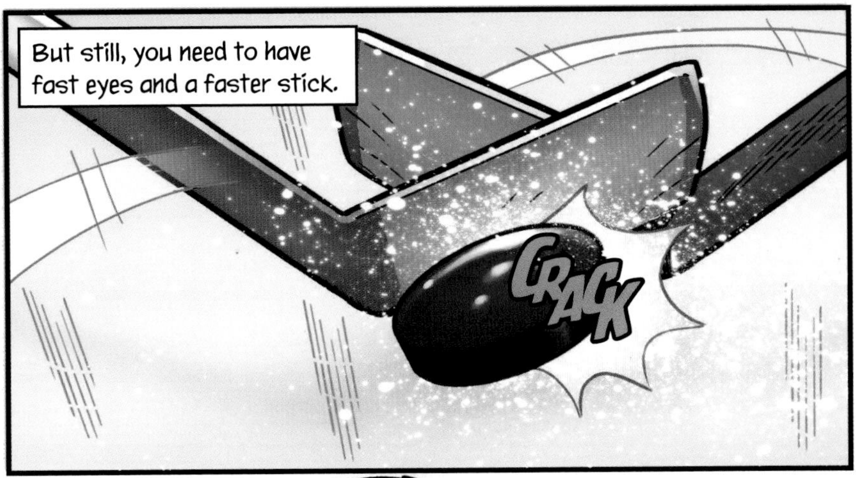
But still, you need to have fast eyes and a faster stick.
CRACK

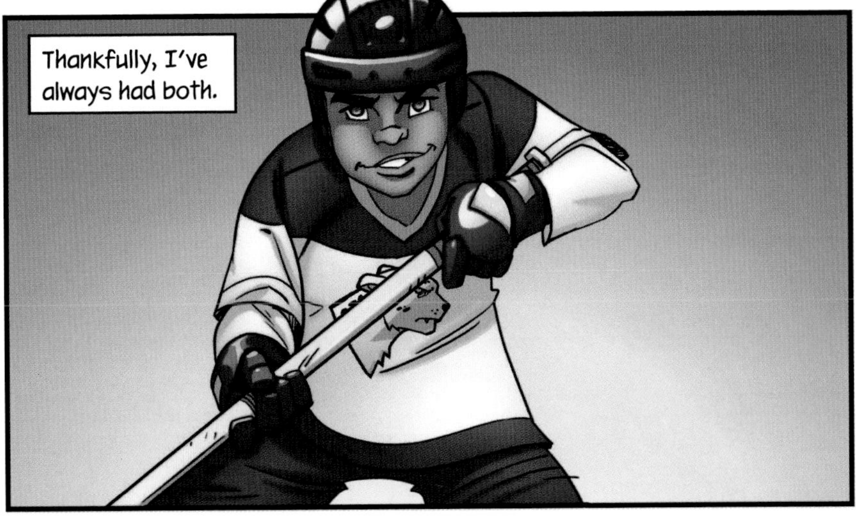
Thankfully, I've always had both.

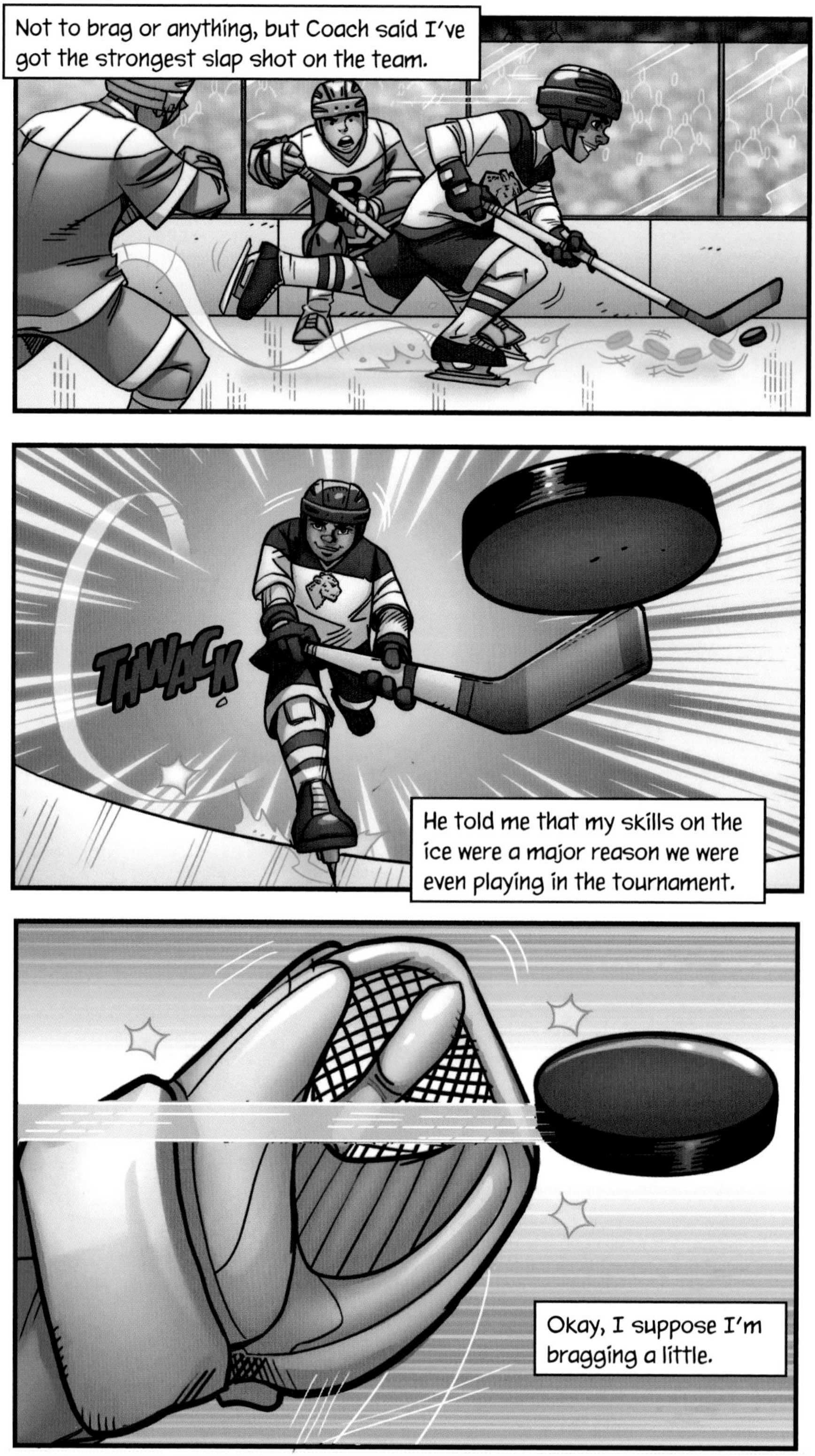
Not to brag or anything, but Coach said I've got the strongest slap shot on the team.
THWACK
He told me that my skills on the ice were a major reason we were even playing in the tournament.
Okay, I suppose I'm bragging a little.

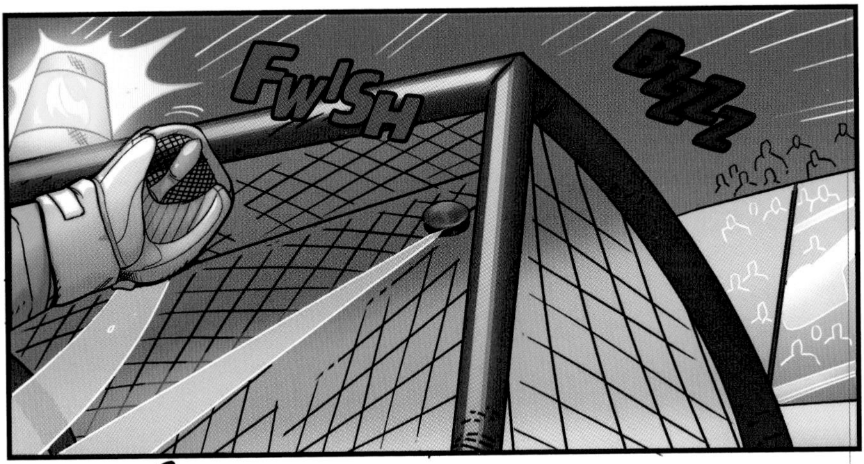
FWISH
BZZZ

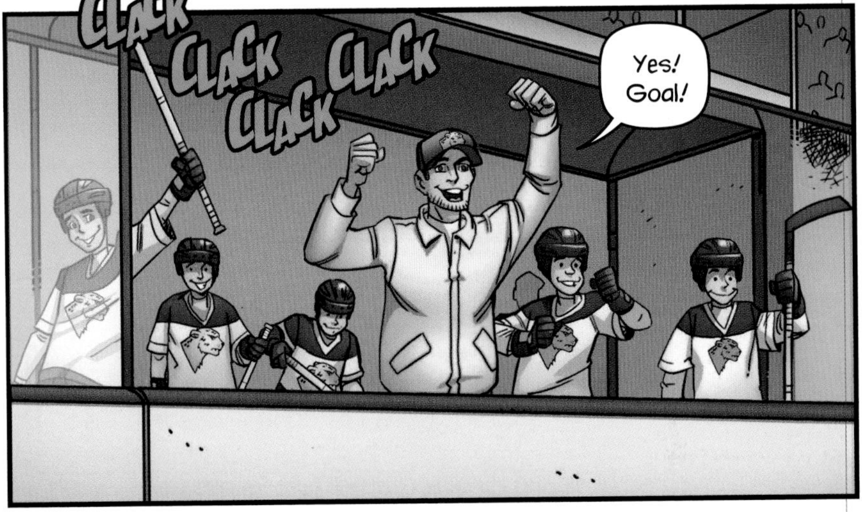
CLACK
CLACK
CLACK
CLACK
Yes! Goal!

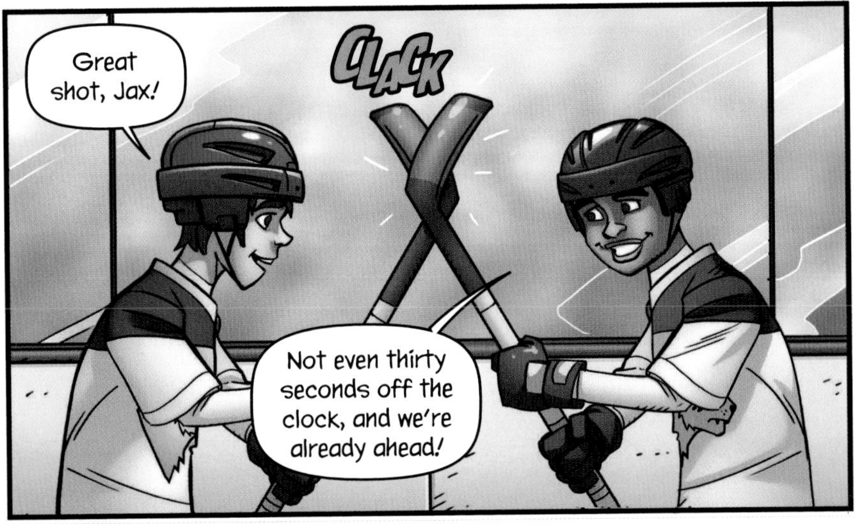
Great shot, Jax!
CLACK
Not even thirty seconds off the clock, and we're already ahead!

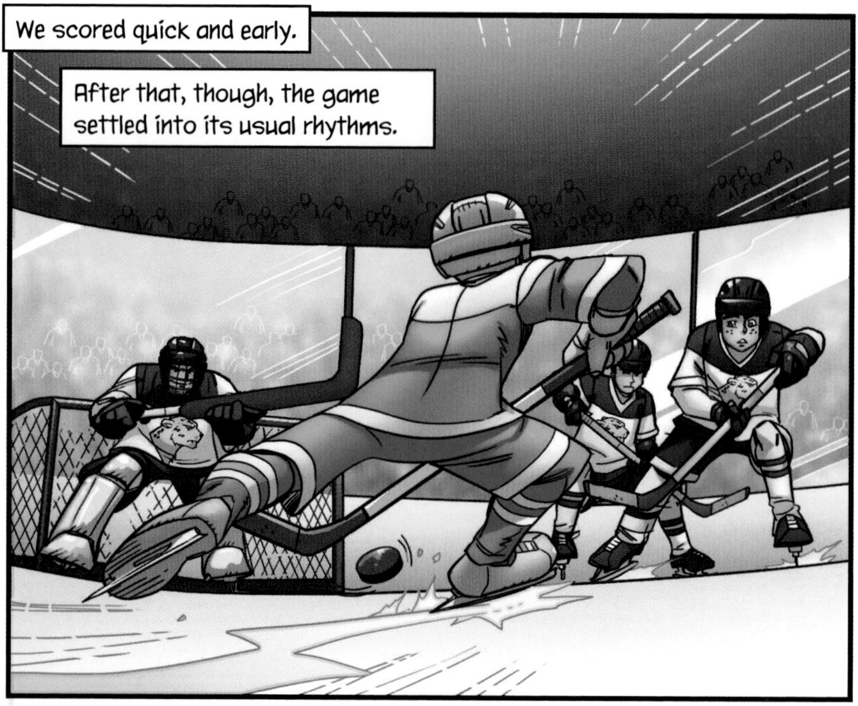
We scored quick and early.
After that, though, the game settled into its usual rhythms.

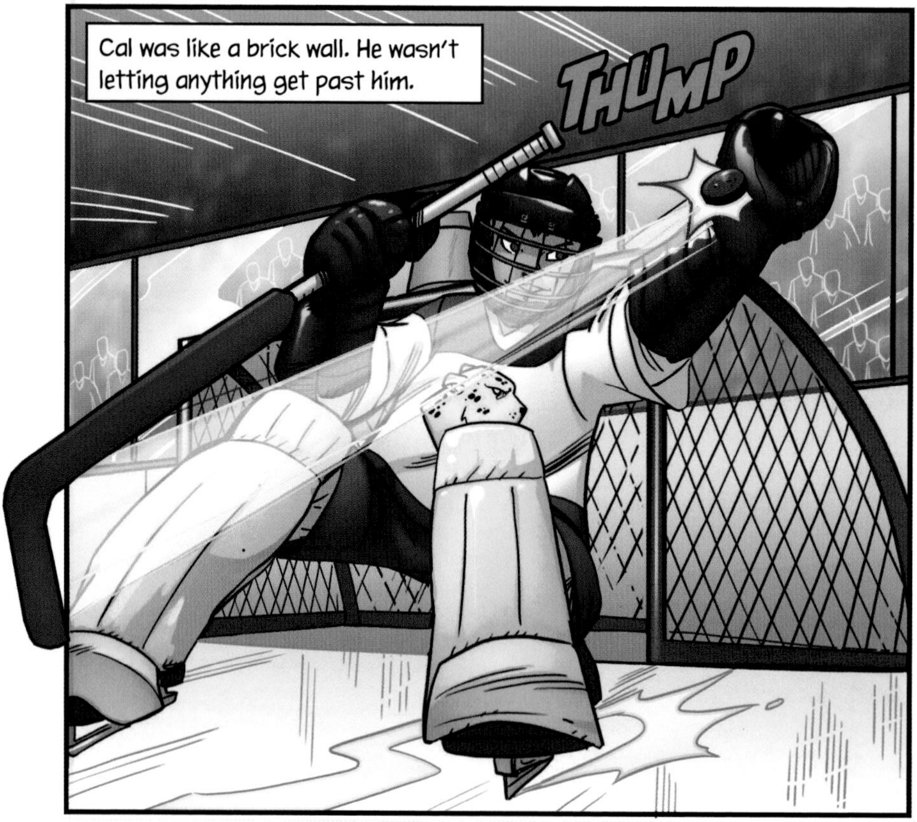
Cal was like a brick wall. He wasn't letting anything get past him.
THUMP

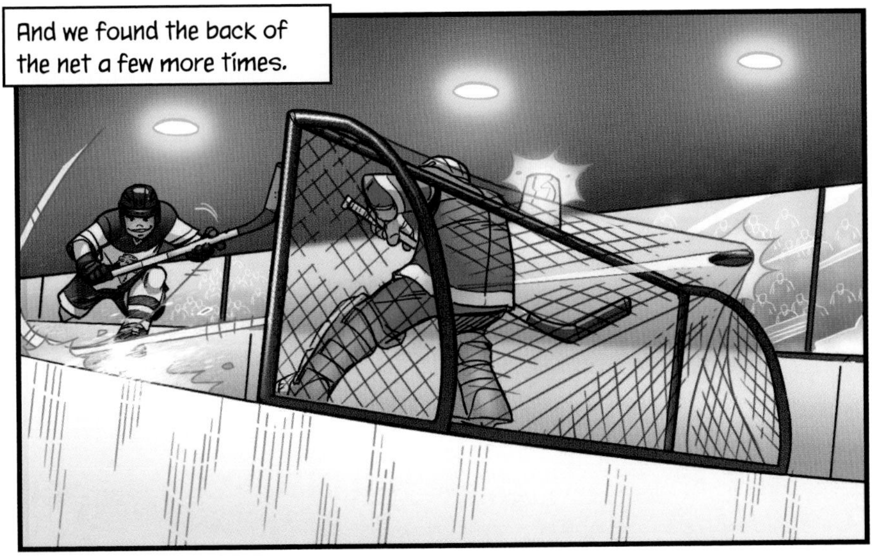
And we found the back of the net a few more times.

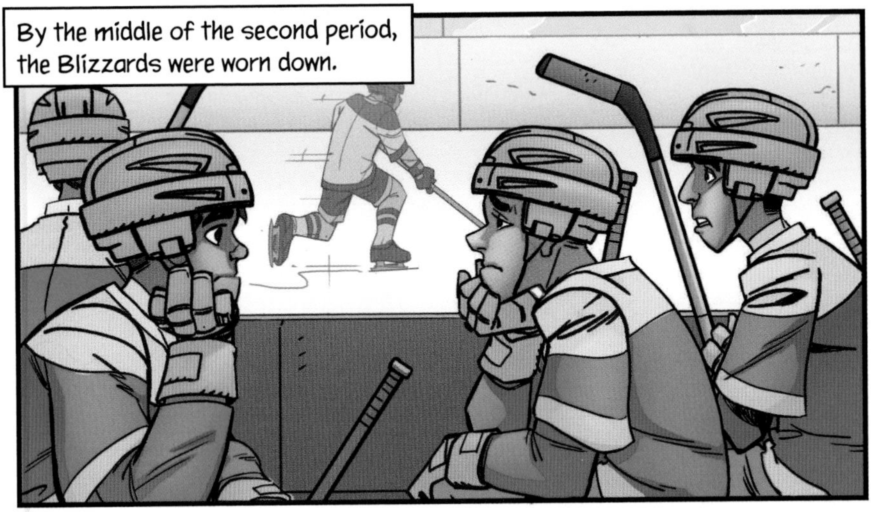
By the middle of the second period, the Blizzards were worn down.

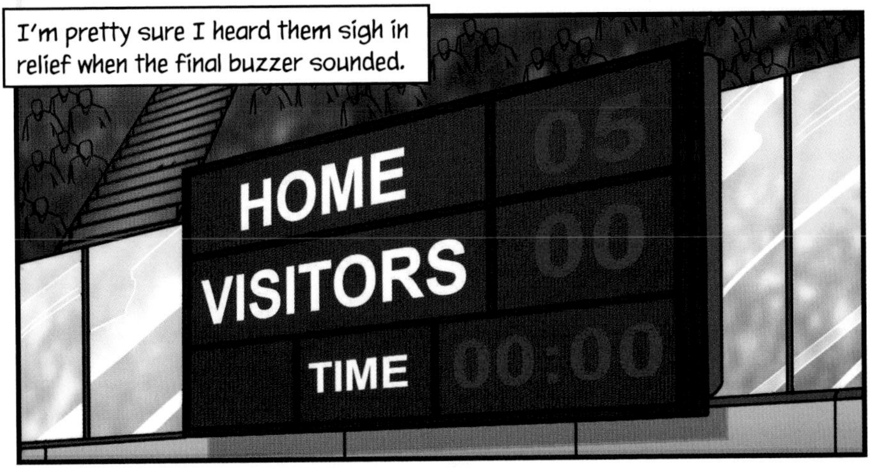
I'm pretty sure I heard them sigh in relief when the final buzzer sounded.
HOME
05
VISITORS
00
TIME
00:00

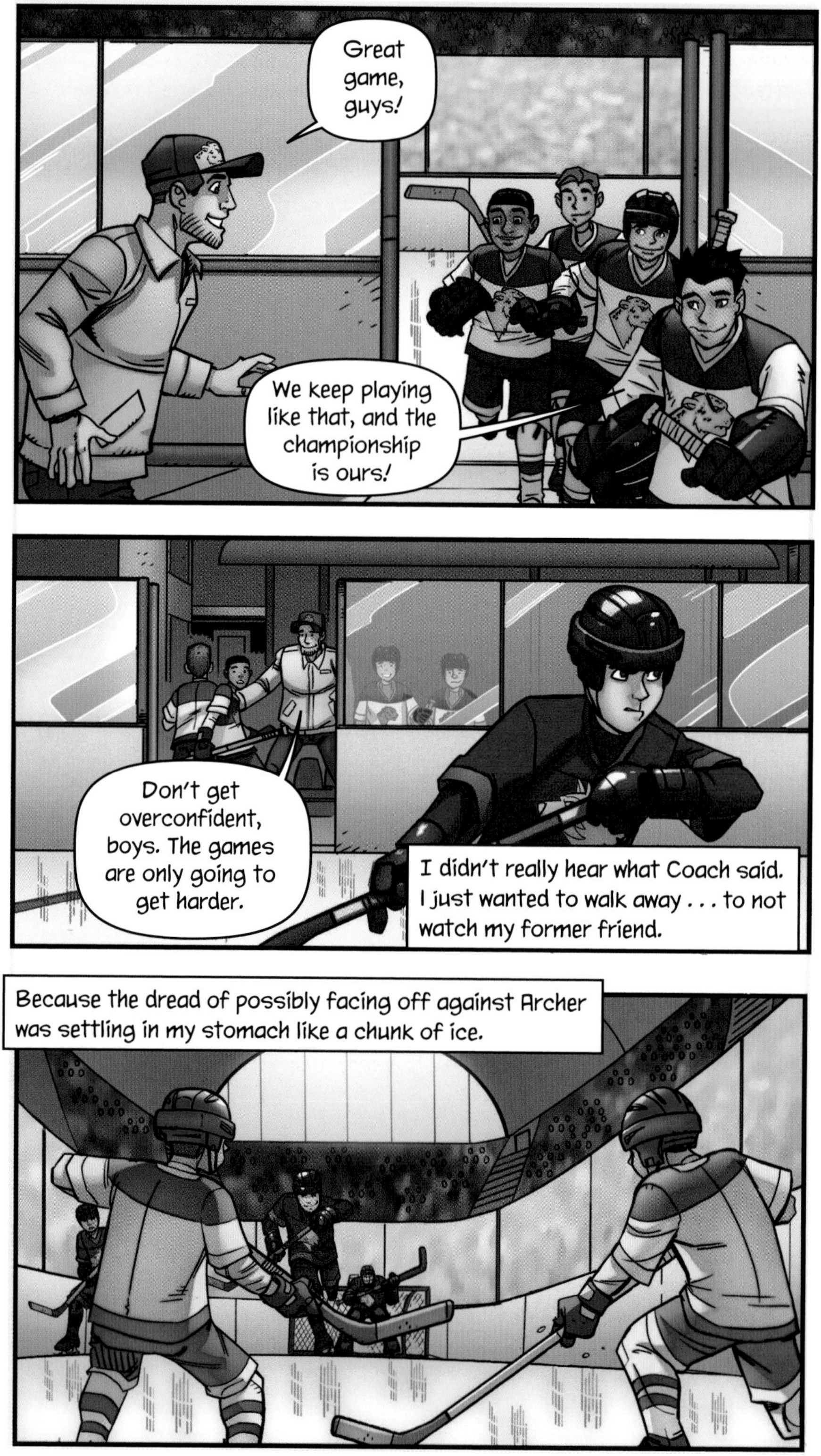

Great game, guys!
We keep playing like that, and the championship is ours!
Don't get overconfident, boys. The games are only going to get harder.
I didn't really hear what Coach said. I just wanted to walk away . . . to not watch my former friend.
Because the dread of possibly facing off against Archer was settling in my stomach like a chunk of ice.

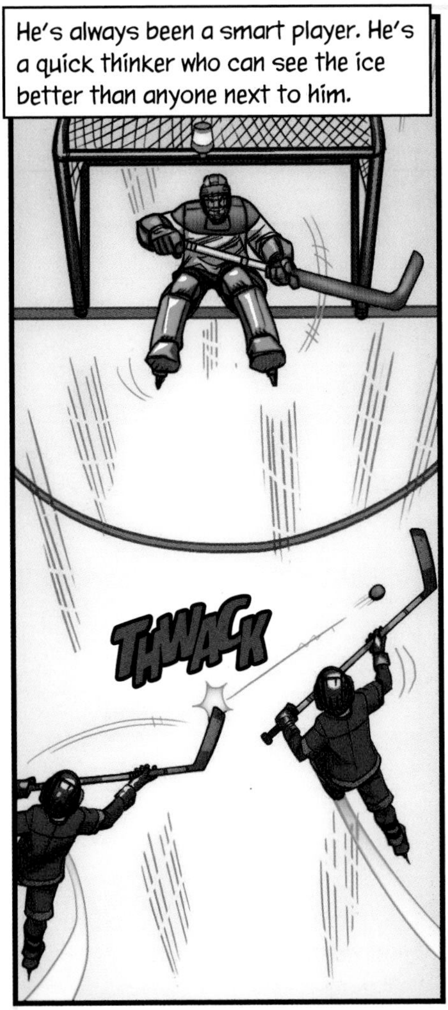
He's always been a smart player. He's a quick thinker who can see the ice better than anyone next to him.
THWACK

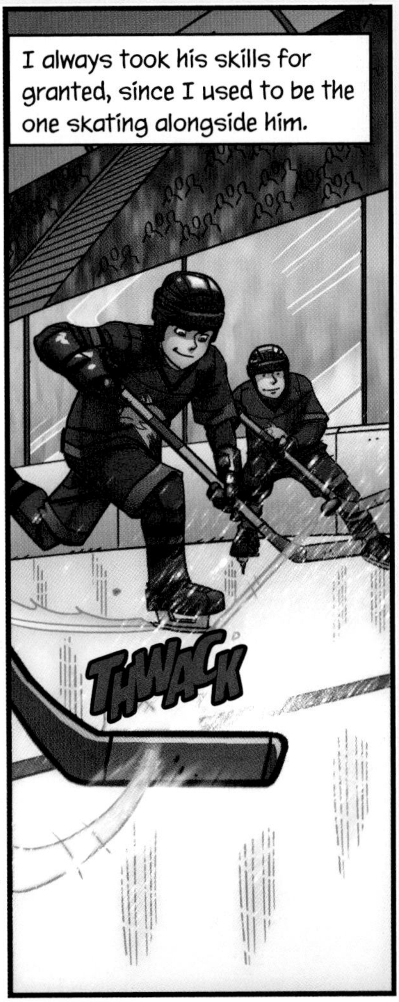
I always took his skills for granted, since I used to be the one skating alongside him.
THWACK

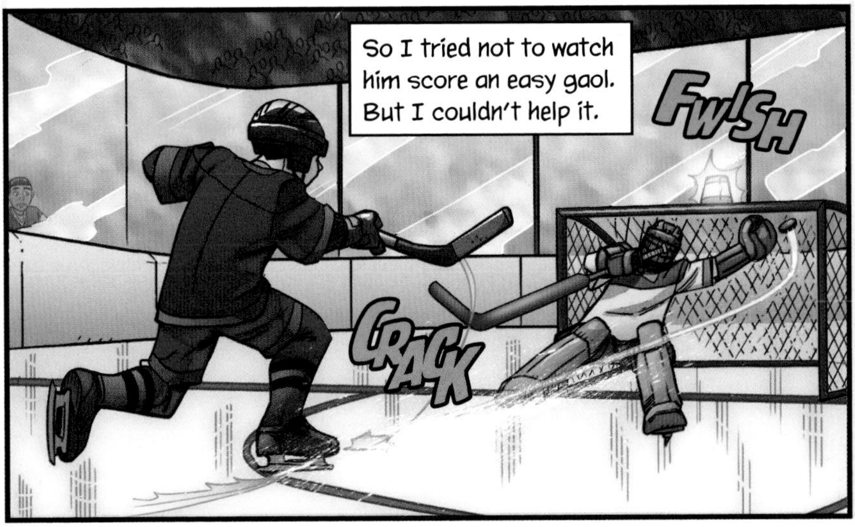
So I tried not to watch him score an easy gaol. But I couldn't help it.
FWISH
CRACK

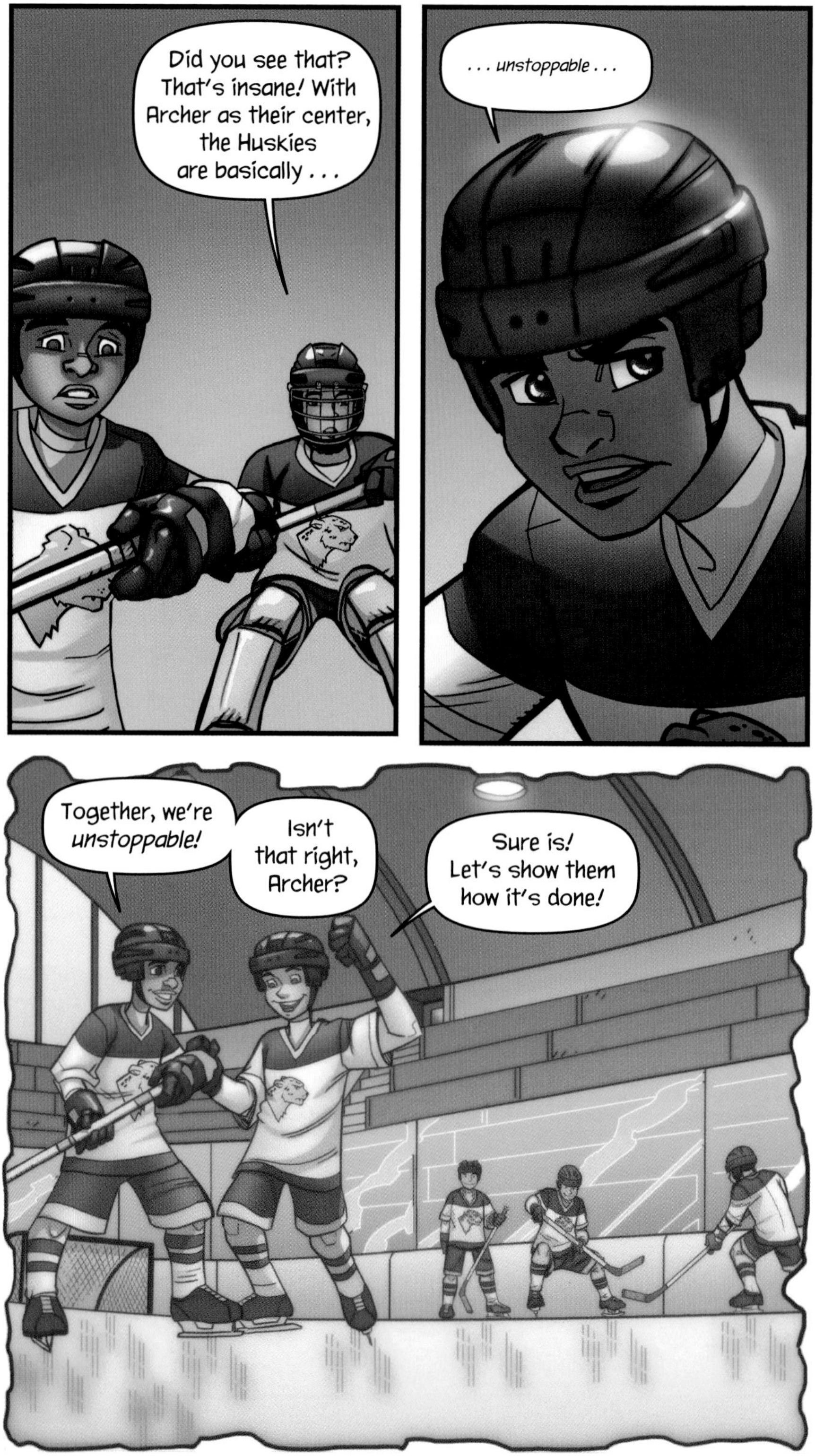
Did you see that? That's insane! With Archer as their center, the Huskies are basically . . .
. . . unstoppable . . .
Together, we're *unstoppable!*
Isn't that right, Archer?
Sure is! Let's show them how it's done!

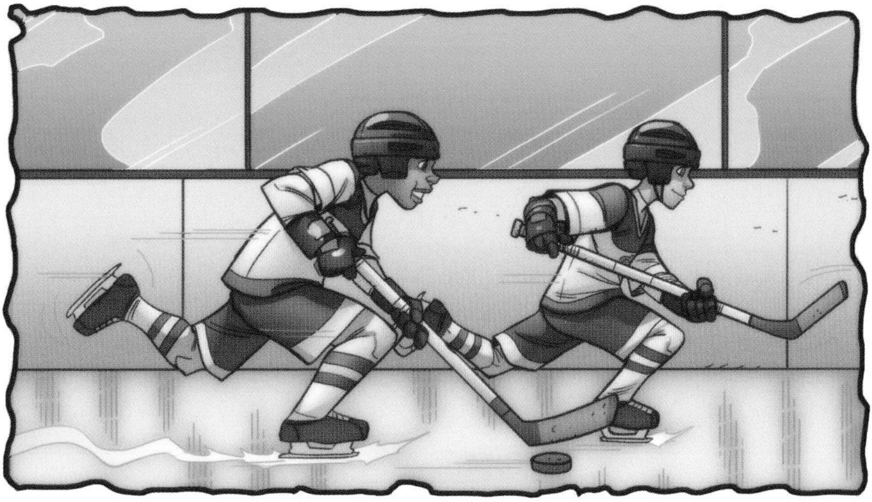

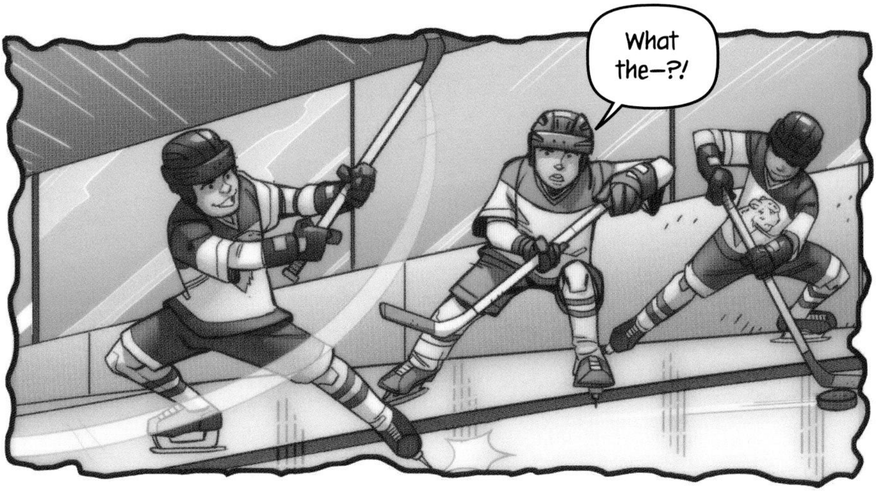
What the–?!

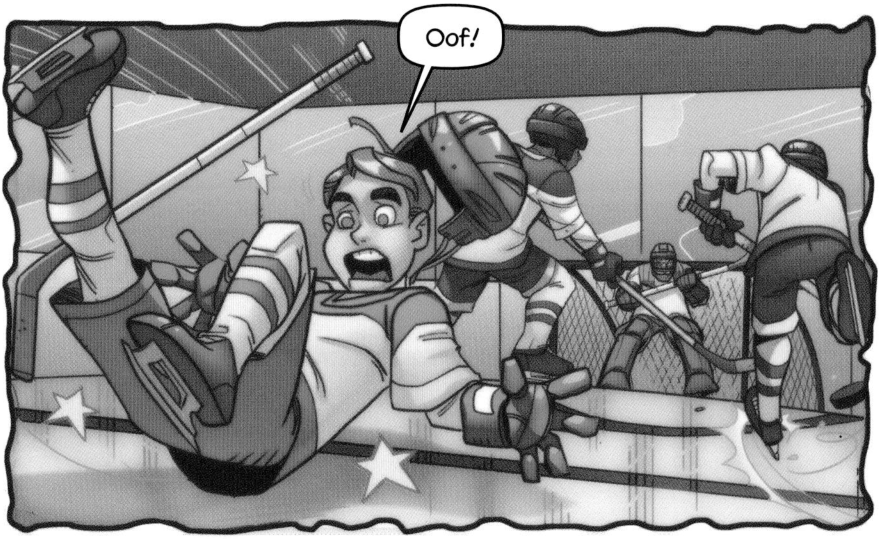
Oof!

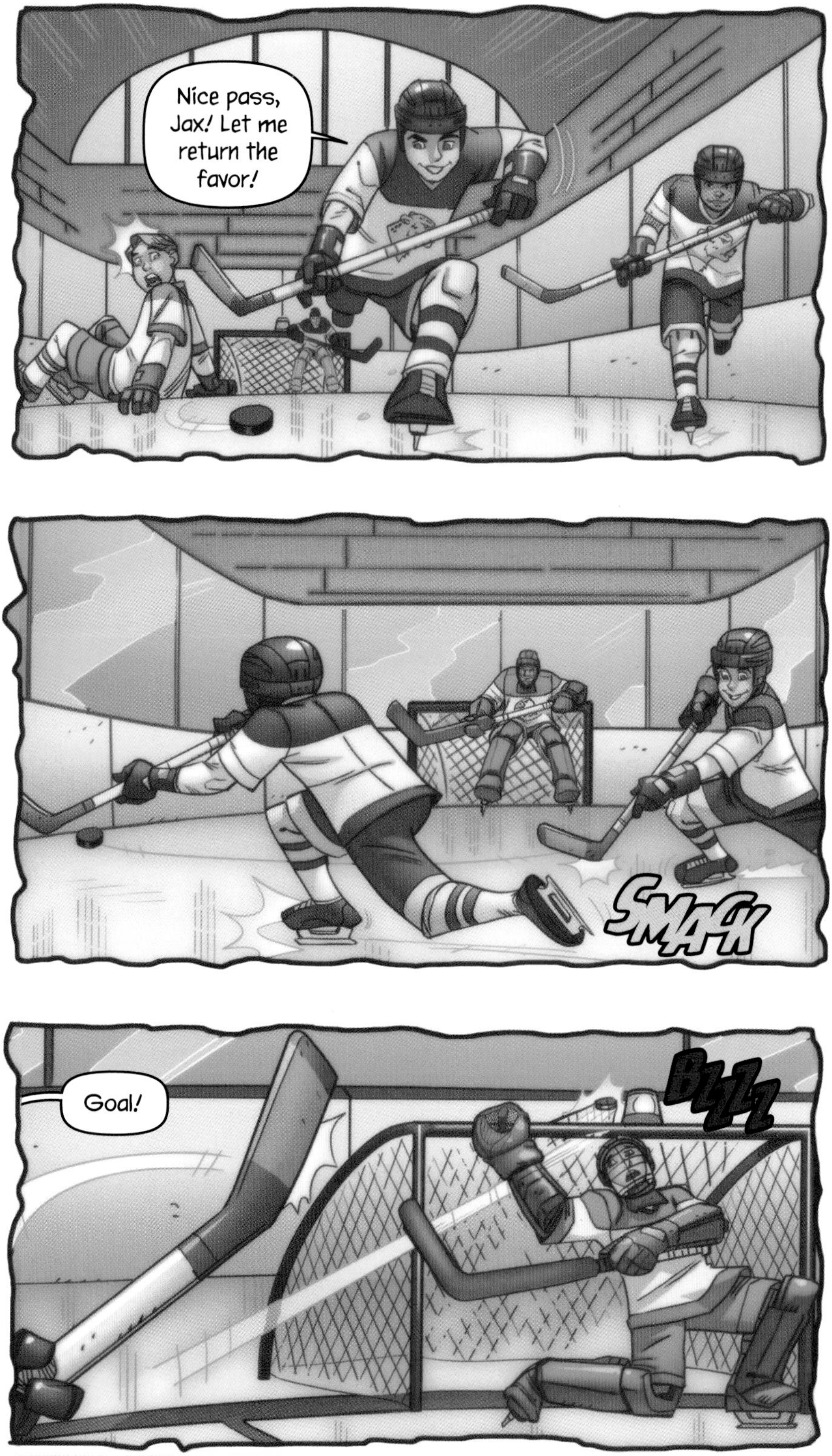
Nice pass, Jax! Let me return the favor!
SMACK
Goal!
BZZZ

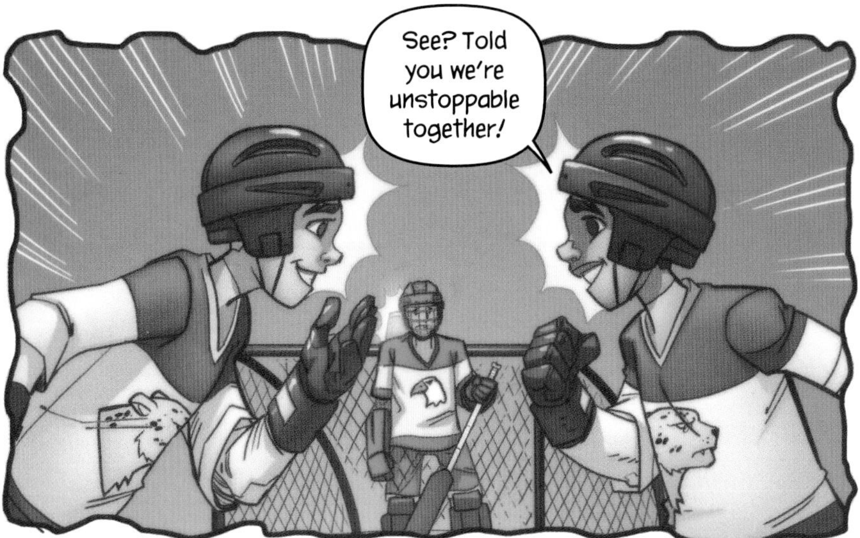
See? Told you we're unstoppable together!

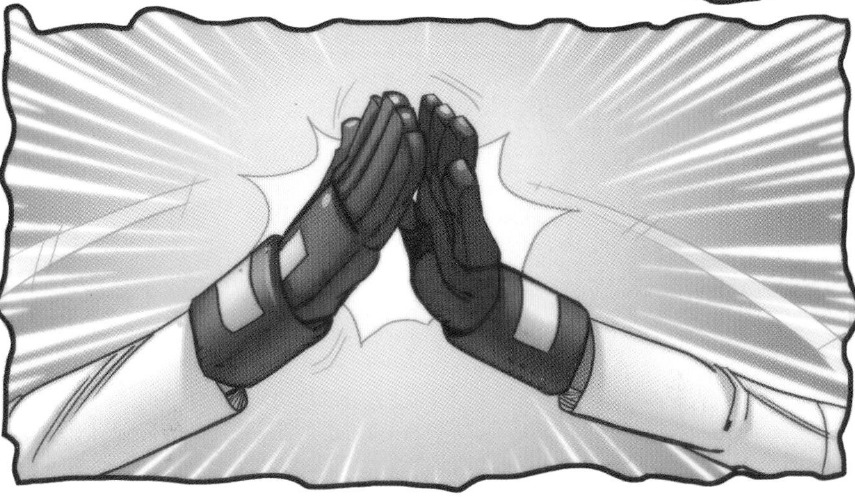

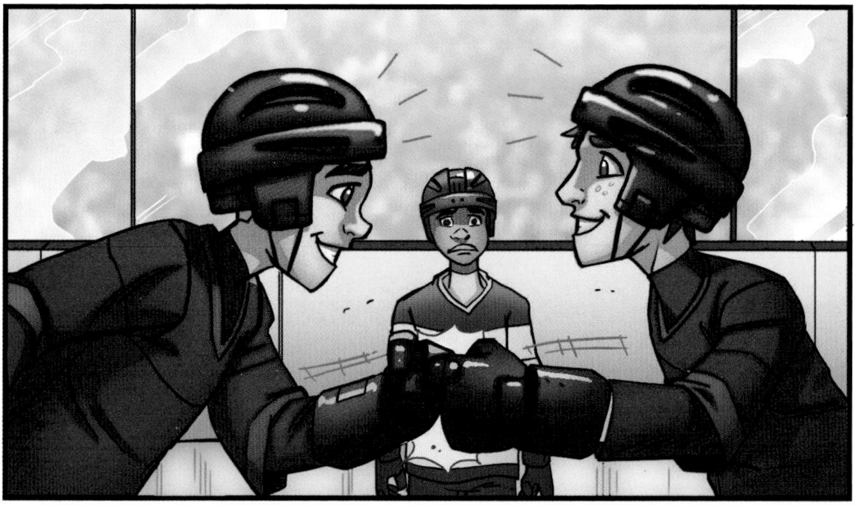

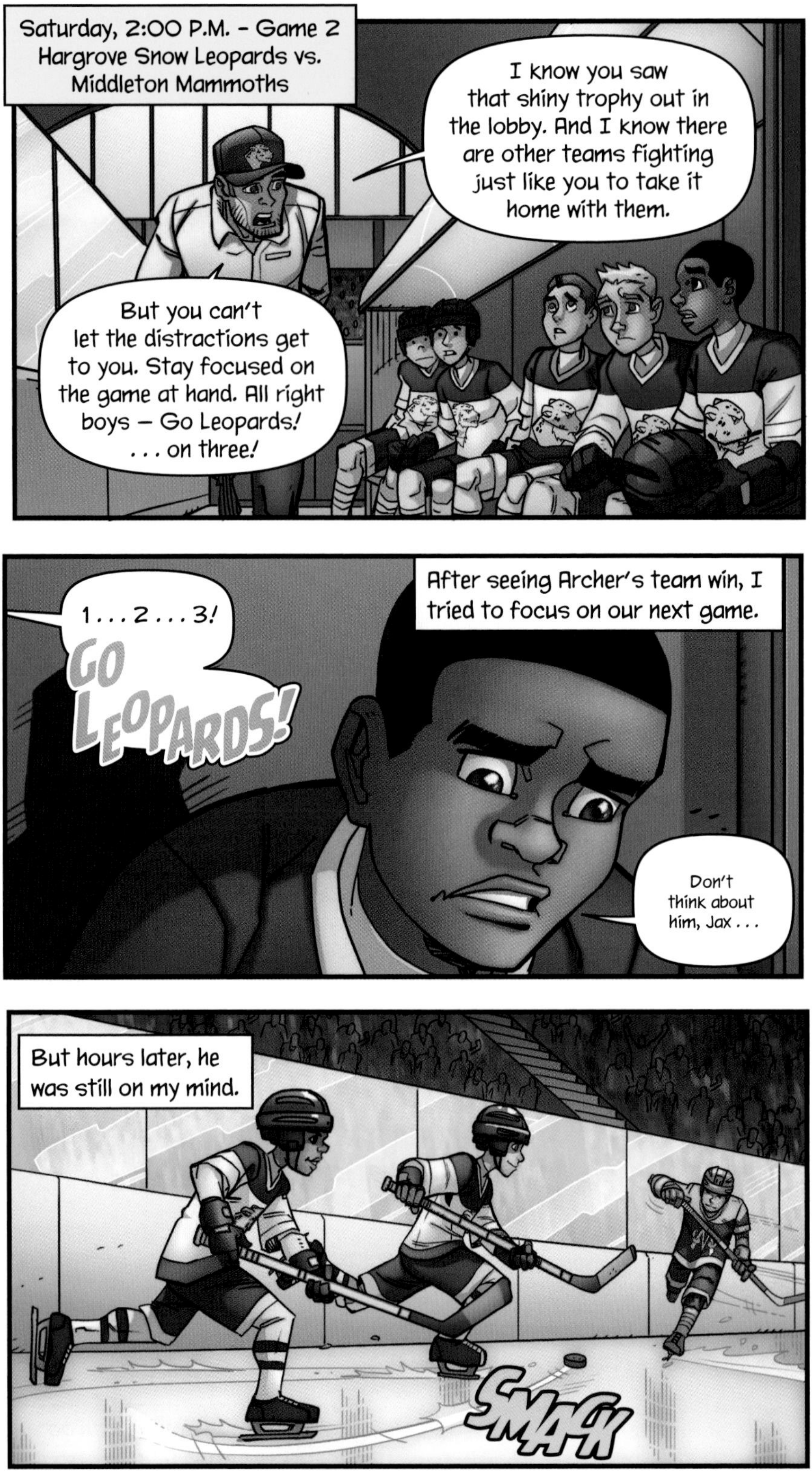
Saturday, 2:00 P.M. – Game 2
Hargrove Snow Leopards vs.
Middleton Mammoths
I know you saw that shiny trophy out in the lobby. And I know there are other teams fighting just like you to take it home with them.
But you can't let the distractions get to you. Stay focused on the game at hand. All right boys – Go Leopards! . . . on three!
After seeing Archer's team win, I tried to focus on our next game.
1 . . . 2 . . . 3!
GO LEOPARDS!
Don't think about him, Jax . . .
But hours later, he was still on my mind.
SMACK

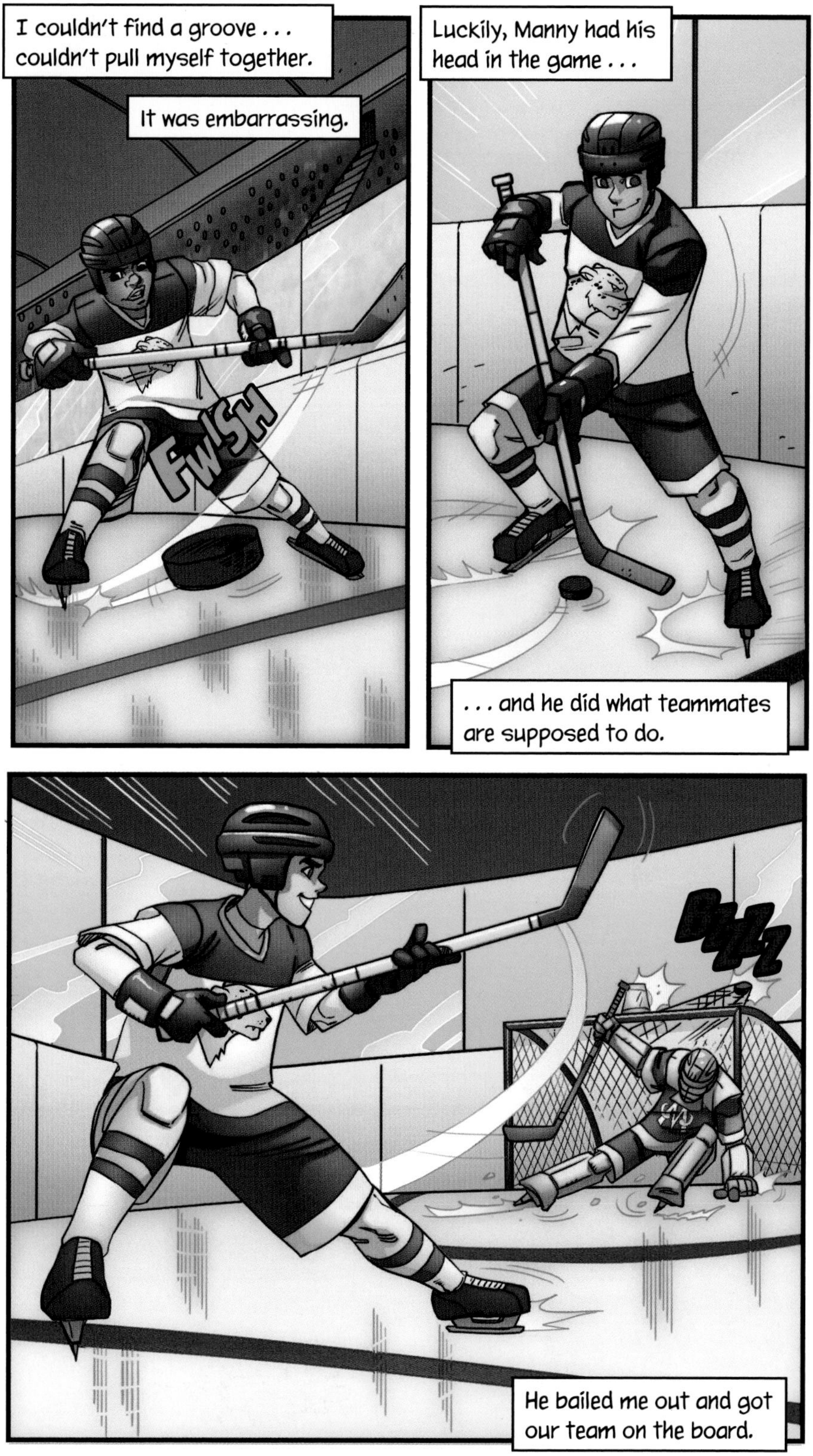
I couldn't find a groove . . . couldn't pull myself together.
It was embarrassing.
FWISH
Luckily, Manny had his head in the game . . .
. . . and he did what teammates are supposed to do.
He bailed me out and got our team on the board.

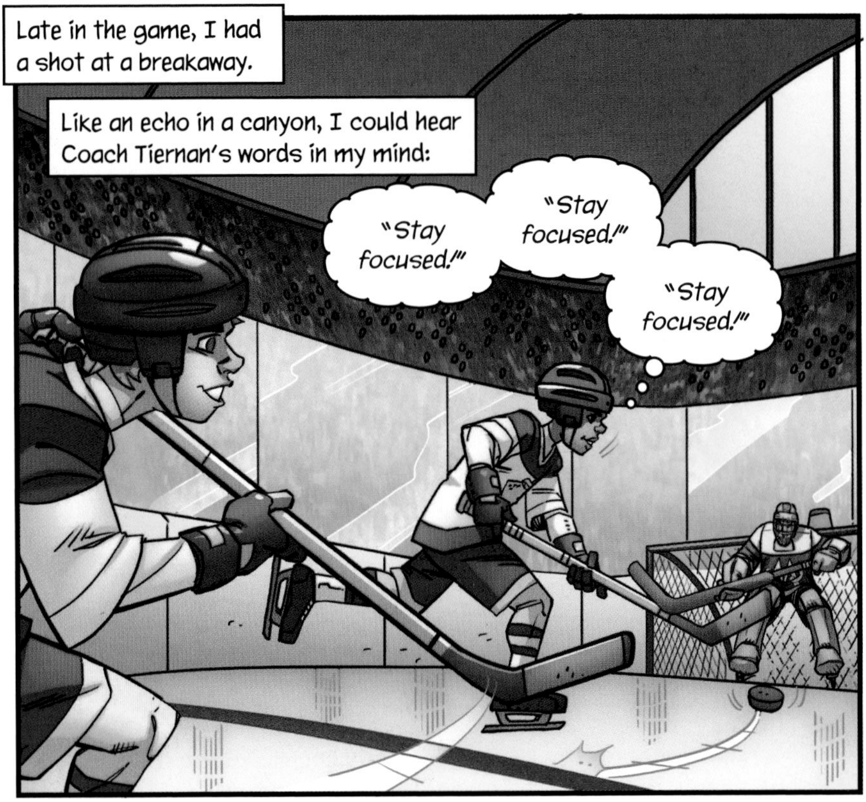
Late in the game, I had a shot at a breakaway.
Like an echo in a canyon, I could hear Coach Tiernan's words in my mind:
"Stay focused!"
"Stay focused!"
"Stay focused!"

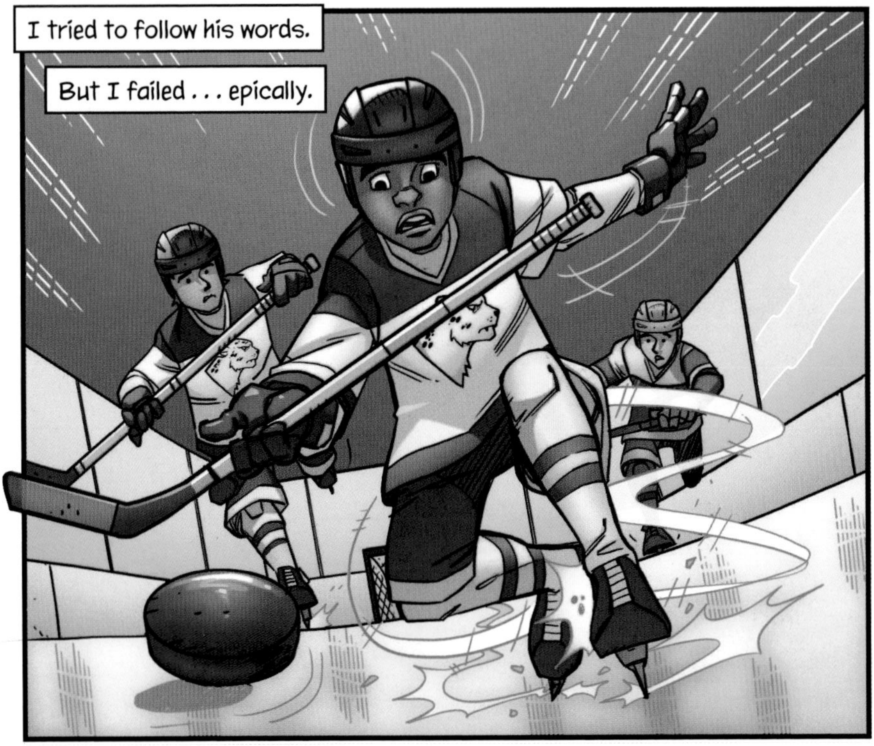
I tried to follow his words.
But I failed . . . epically.

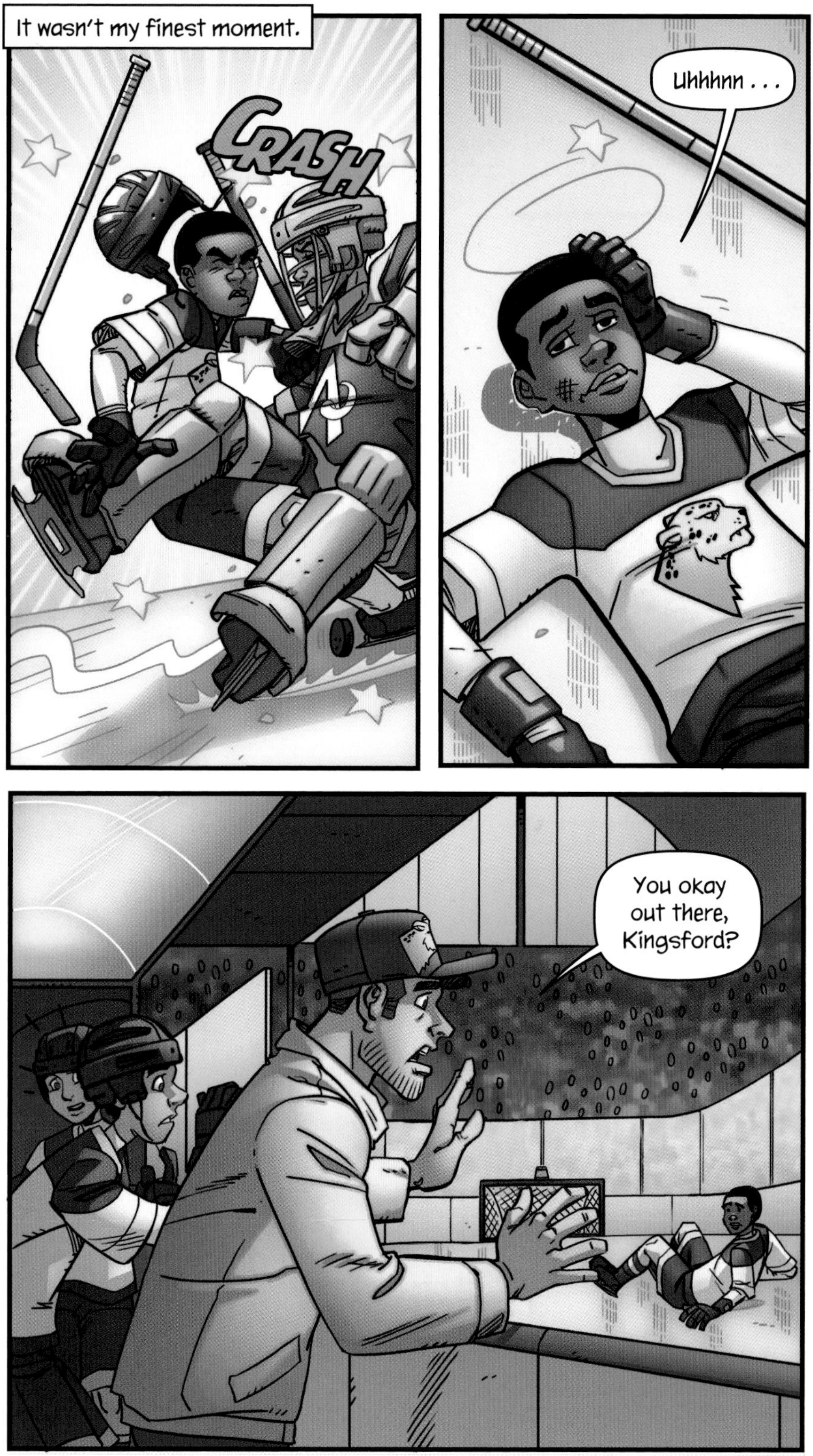
It wasn't my finest moment.
CRASH
Uhhhnn . . .
You okay out there, Kingsford?

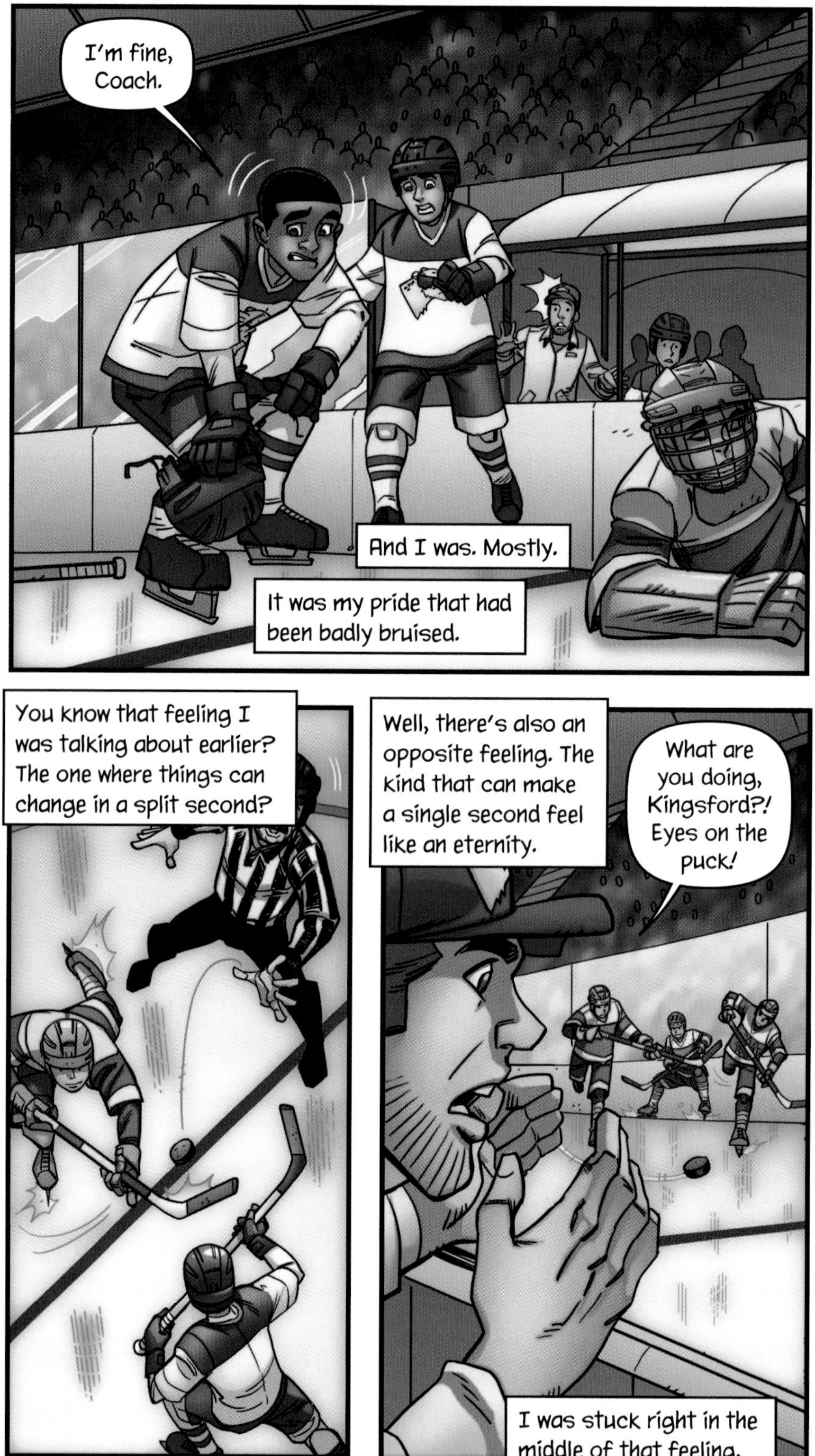
I'm fine, Coach.
And I was. Mostly.
It was my pride that had been badly bruised.
You know that feeling I was talking about earlier? The one where things can change in a split second?
Well, there's also an opposite feeling. The kind that can make a single second feel like an eternity.
What are you doing, Kingsford?! Eyes on the puck!
I was stuck right in the middle of that feeling.

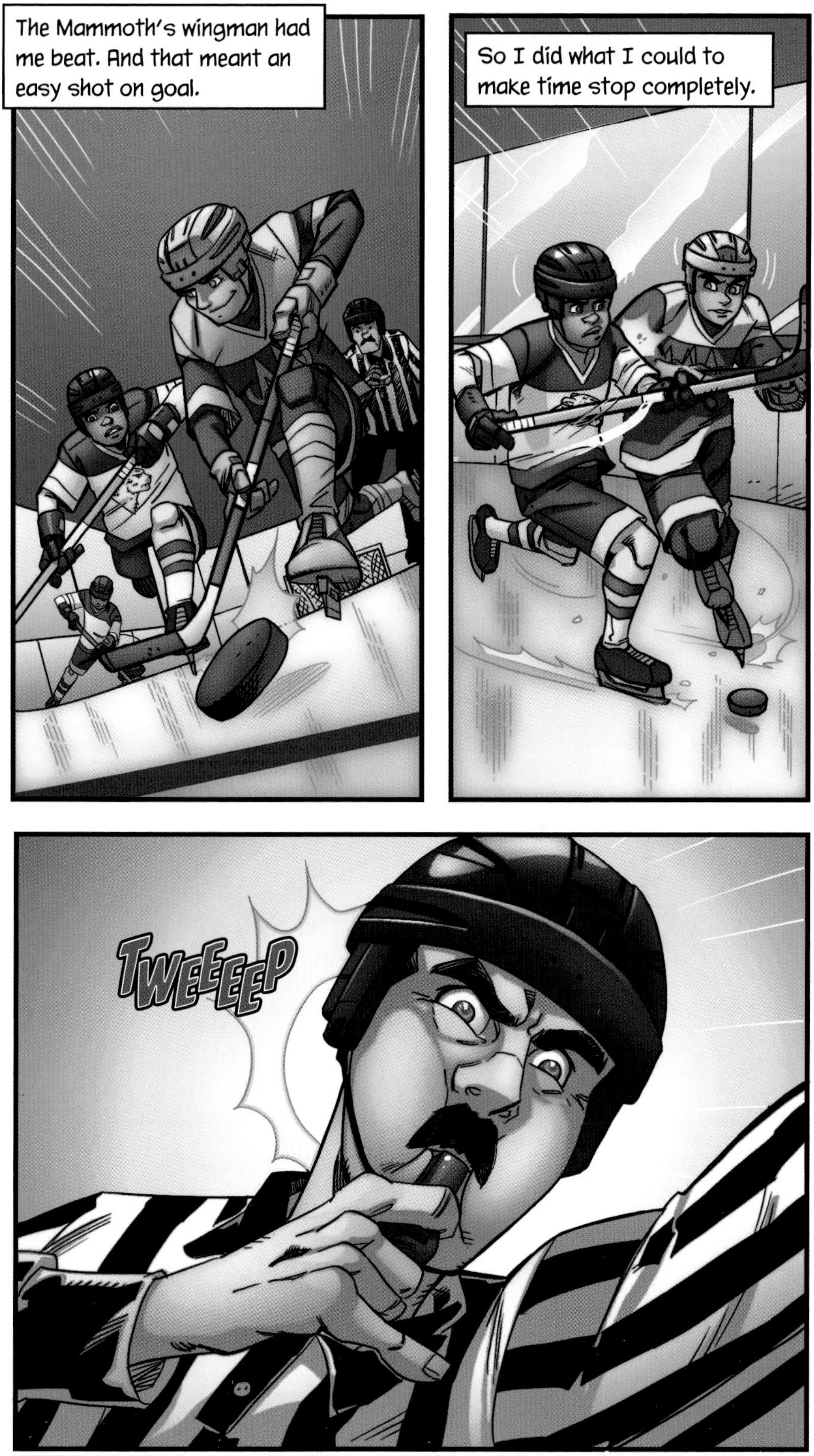
The Mammoth's wingman had me beat. And that meant an easy shot on goal.
So I did what I could to make time stop completely.
TWEEEEP

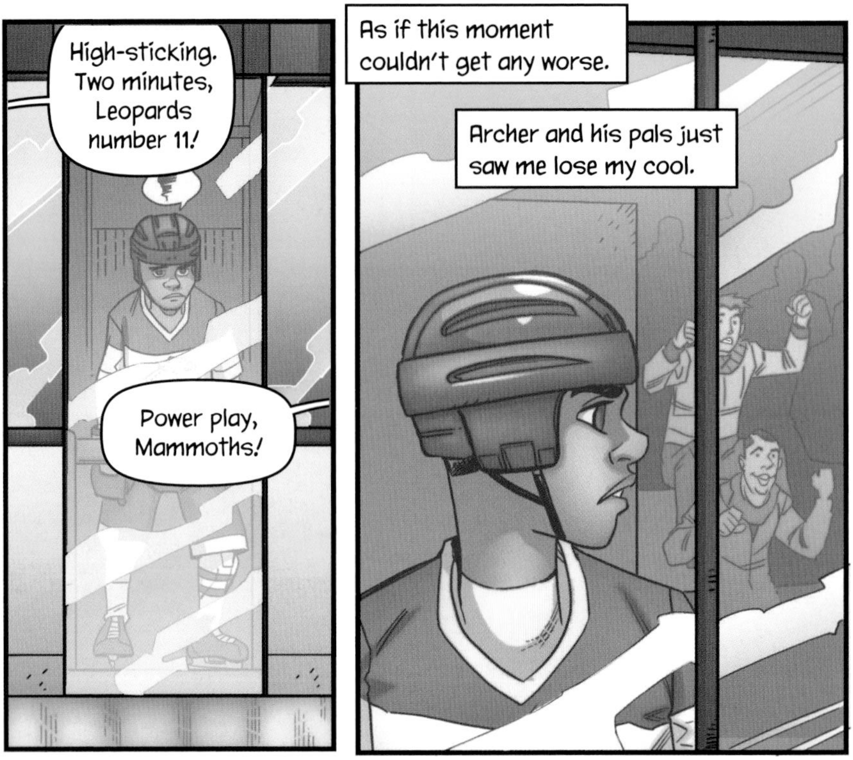
High-sticking. Two minutes, Leopards number 11!
Power play, Mammoths!
As if this moment couldn't get any worse.
Archer and his pals just saw me lose my cool.

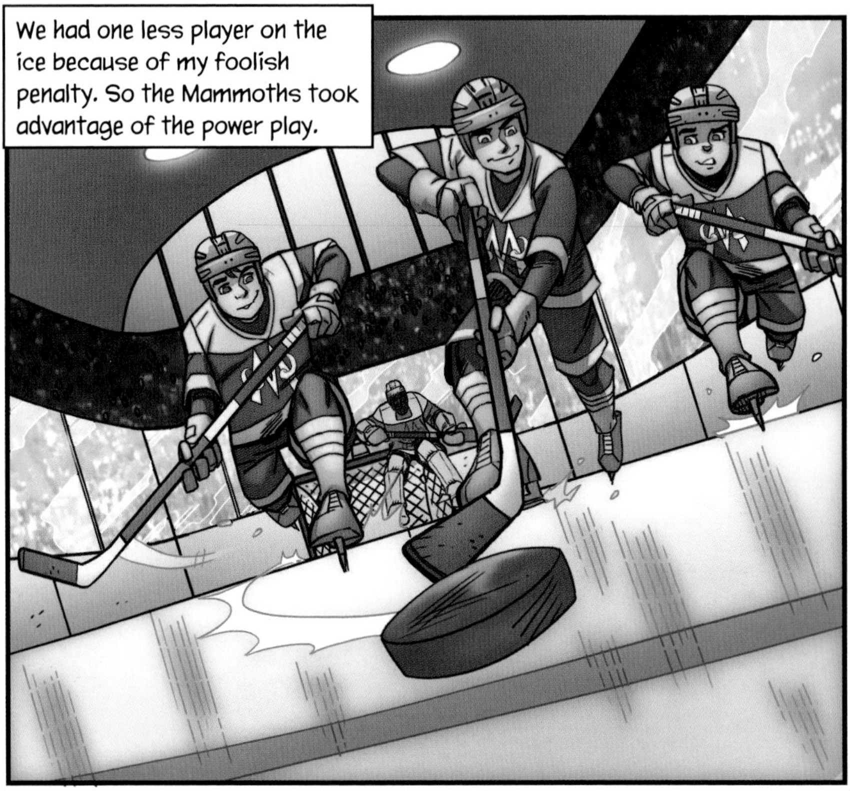
We had one less player on the ice because of my foolish penalty. So the Mammoths took advantage of the power play.

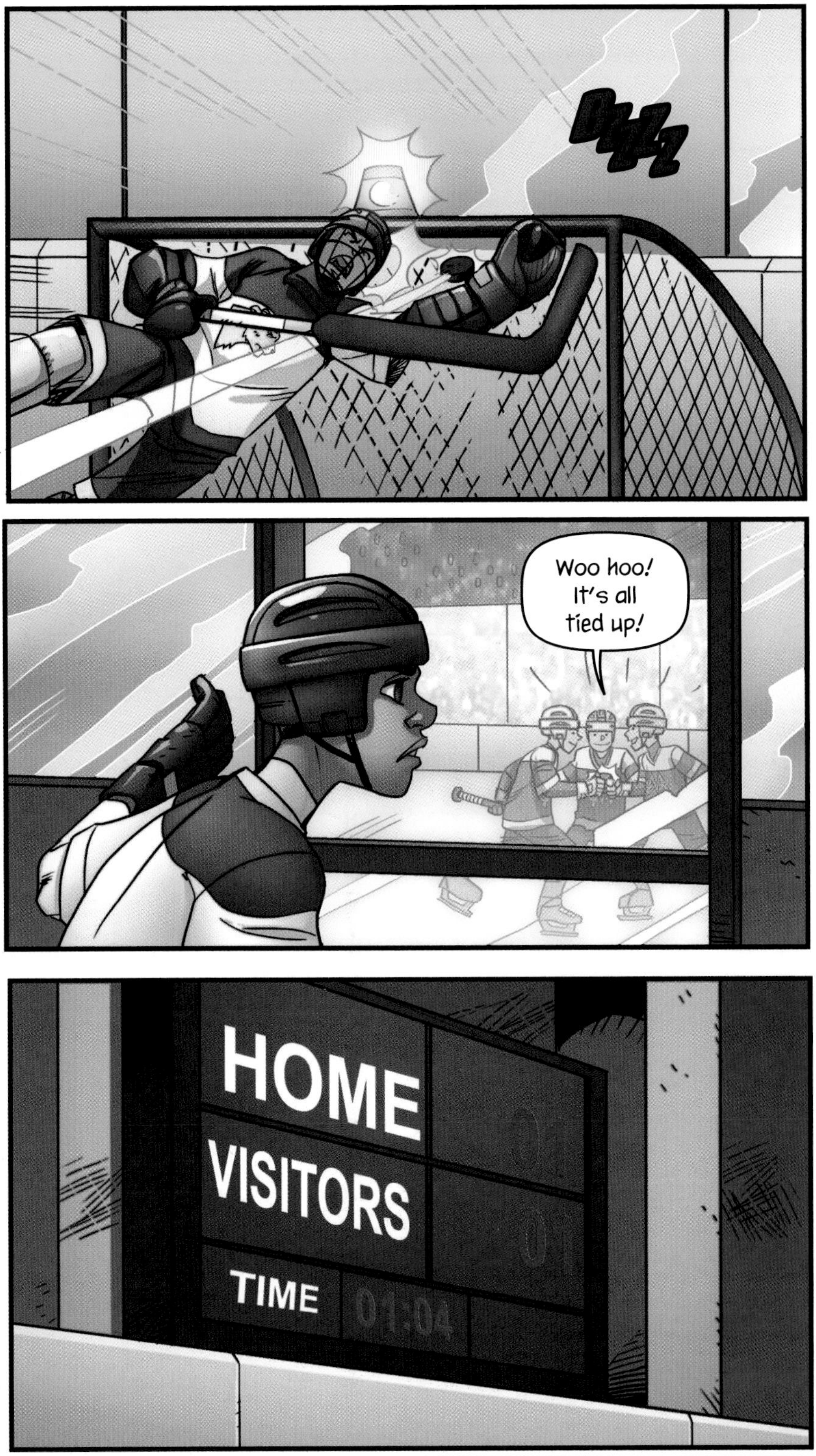
Woo hoo! It's all tied up!
HOME
VISITORS
TIME
01:04

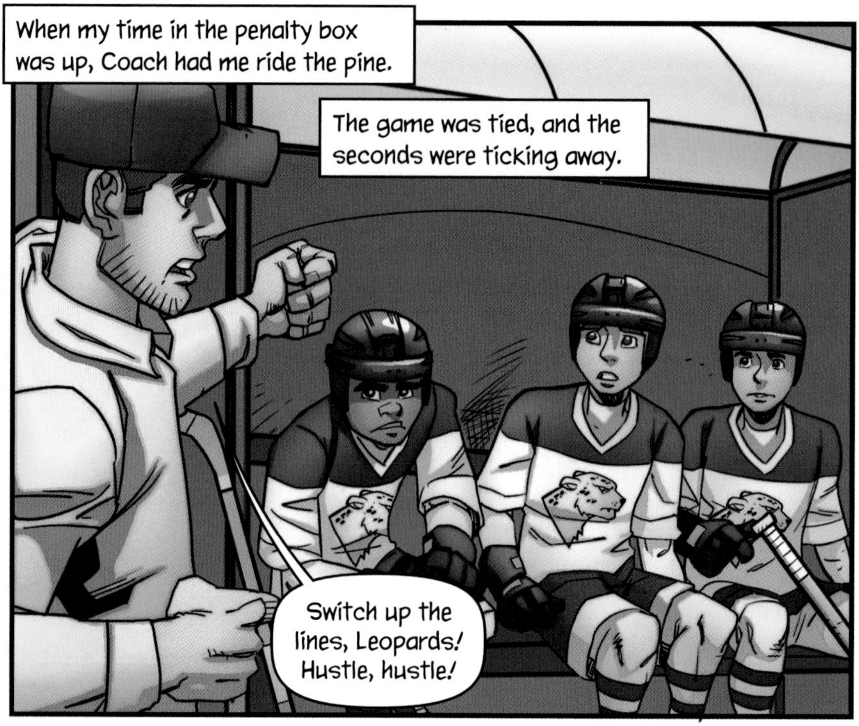
When my time in the penalty box was up, Coach had me ride the pine.
The game was tied, and the seconds were ticking away.
Switch up the lines, Leopards! Hustle, hustle!

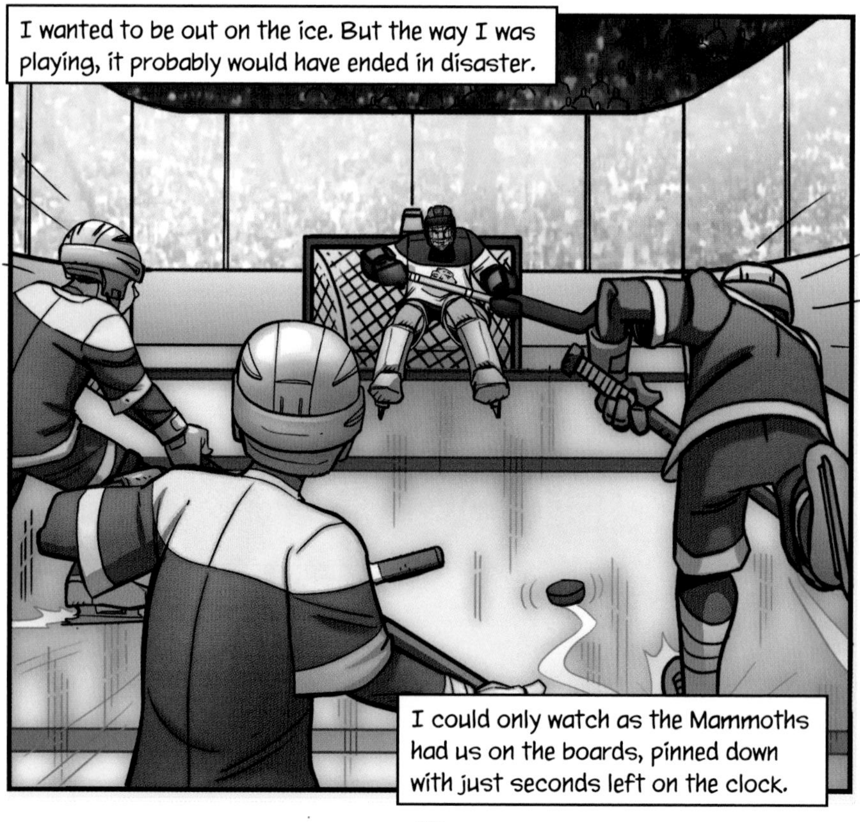
I wanted to be out on the ice. But the way I was playing, it probably would have ended in disaster.
I could only watch as the Mammoths had us on the boards, pinned down with just seconds left on the clock.

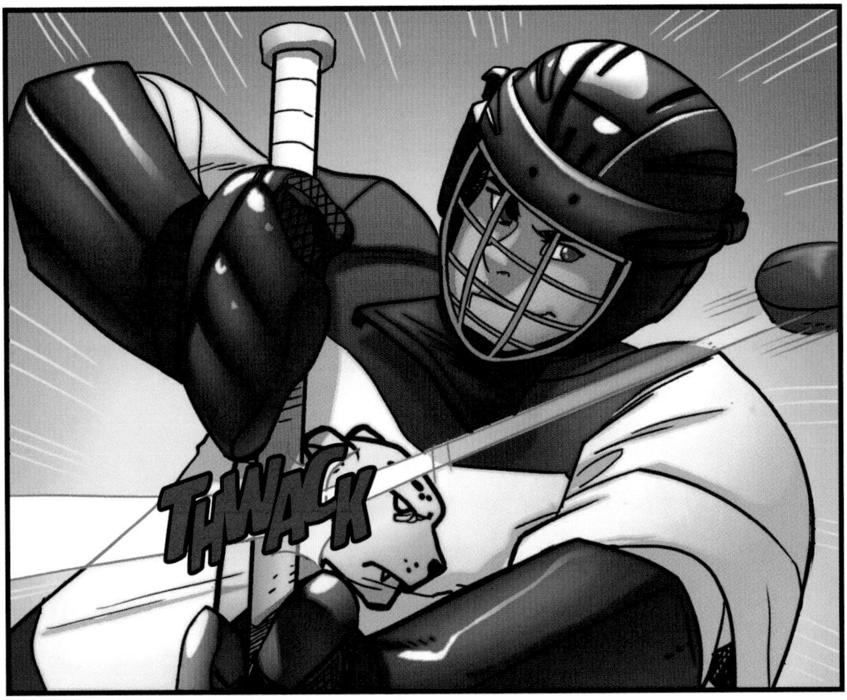
THWACK

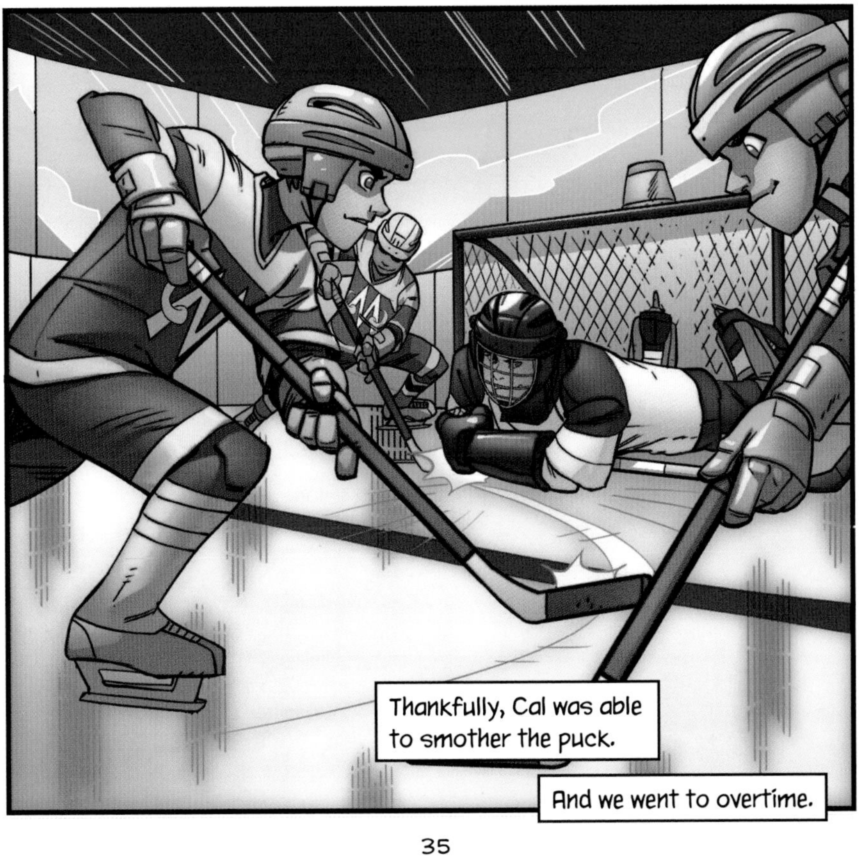
Thankfully, Cal was able to smother the puck.
And we went to overtime.

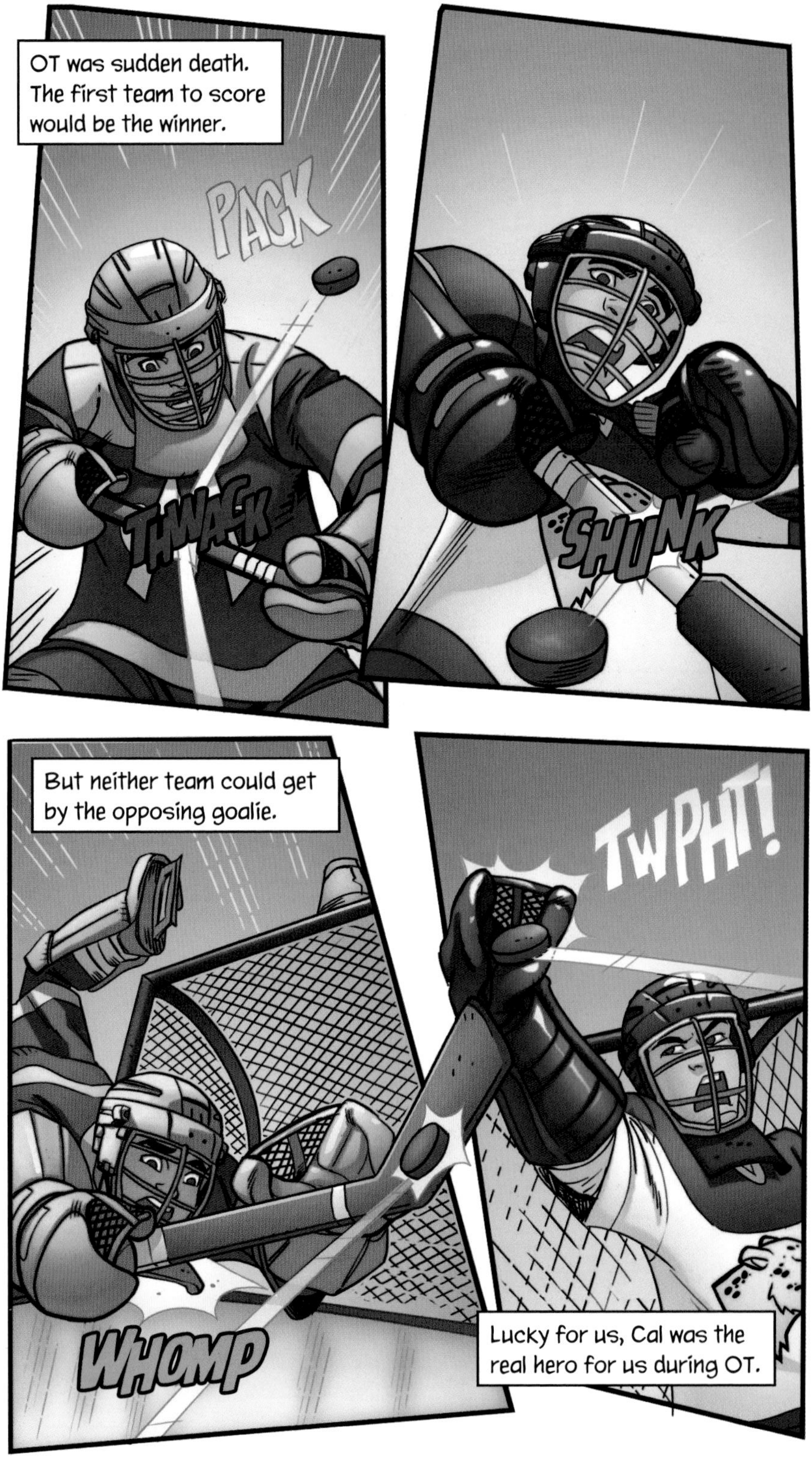
OT was sudden death. The first team to score would be the winner.
PACK
THWACK
SHUNK
But neither team could get by the opposing goalie.
TWPHT!
WHOMP
Lucky for us, Cal was the real hero for us during OT.

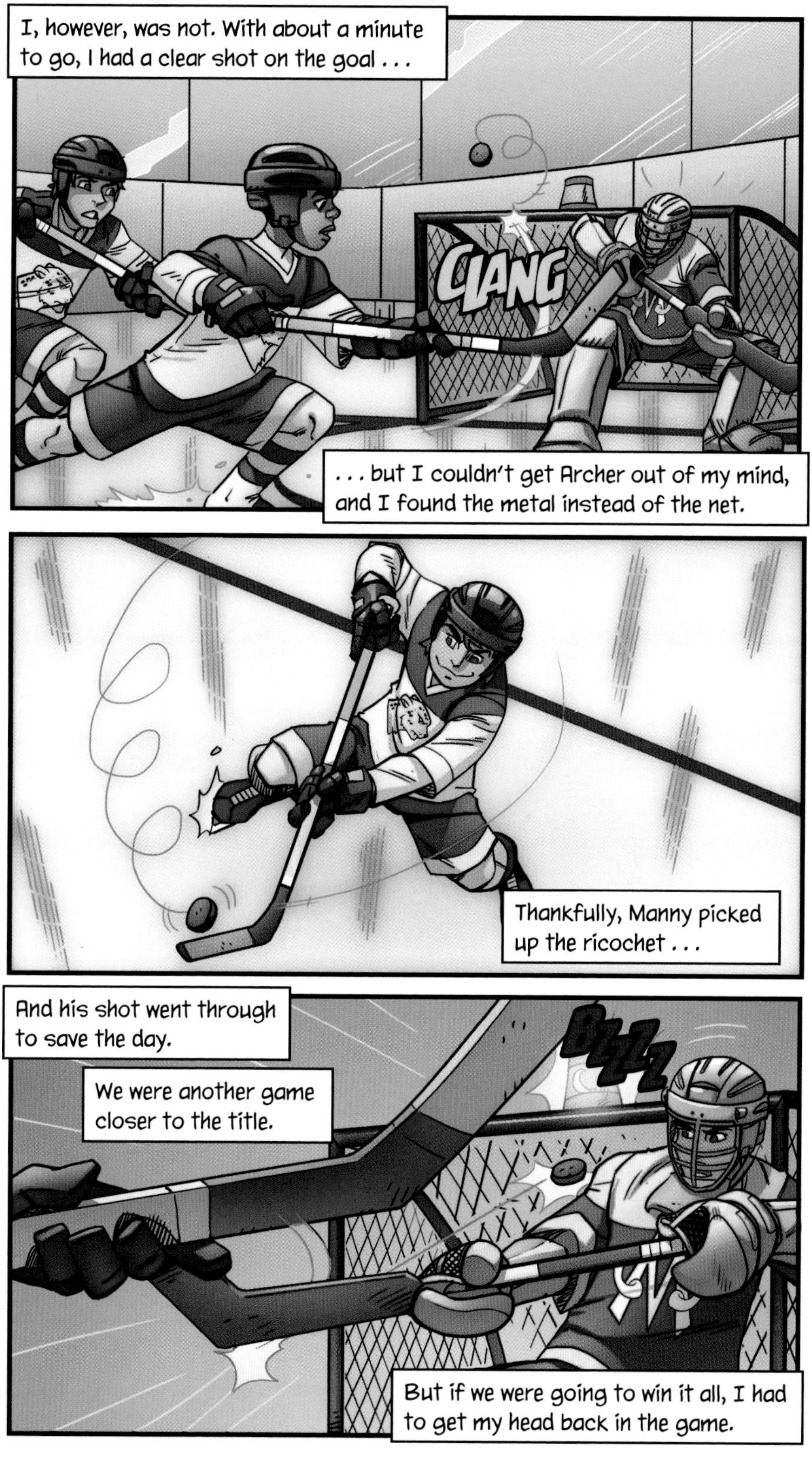
I, however, was not. With about a minute to go, I had a clear shot on the goal . . .
CLANG
. . . but I couldn't get Archer out of my mind, and I found the metal instead of the net.
Thankfully, Manny picked up the ricochet . . .
And his shot went through to save the day.
We were another game closer to the title.
But if we were going to win it all, I had to get my head back in the game.

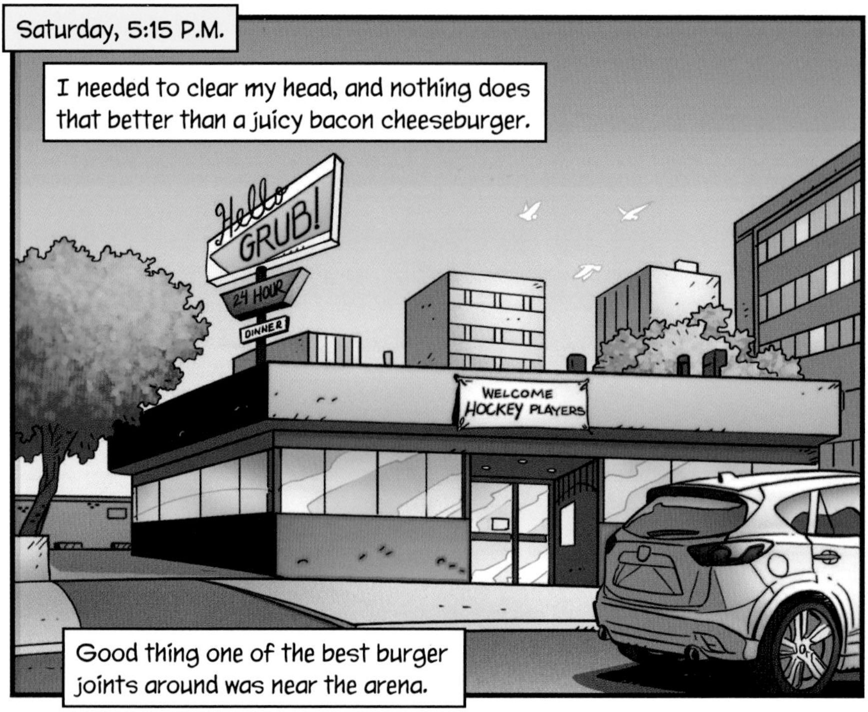
Saturday, 5:15 P.M.
I needed to clear my head, and nothing does that better than a juicy bacon cheeseburger.
Hello GRUB!
24 HOUR
DINNER
WELCOME HOCKEY PLAYERS
Good thing one of the best burger joints around was near the arena.

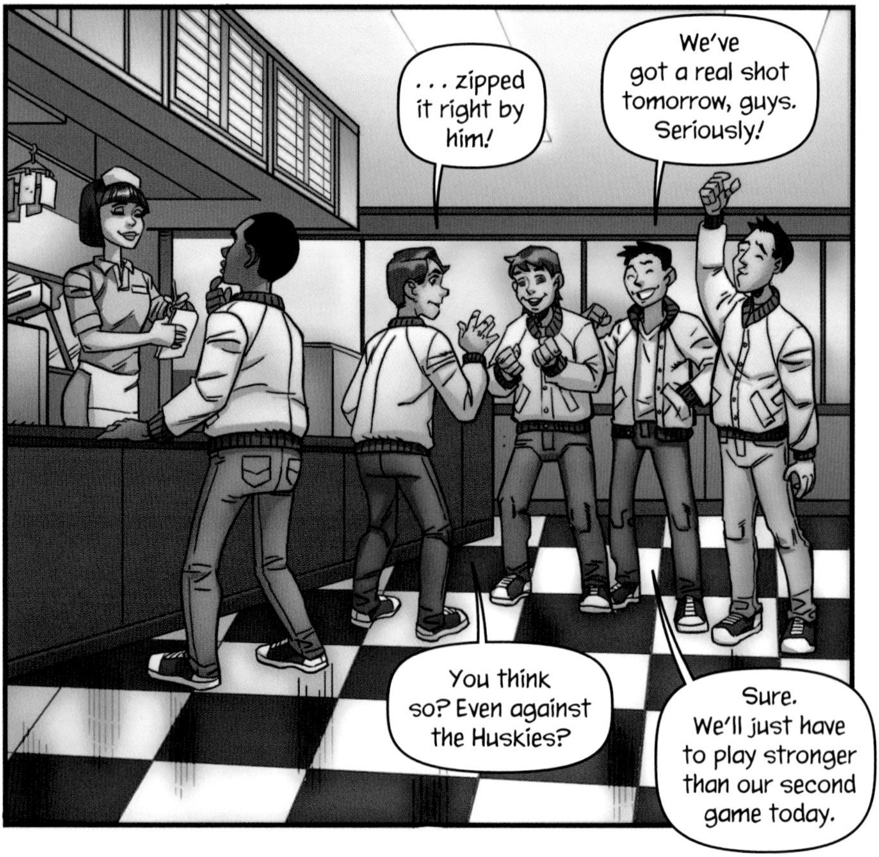
. . . zipped it right by him!
We've got a real shot tomorrow, guys. Seriously!
You think so? Even against the Huskies?
Sure. We'll just have to play stronger than our second game today.

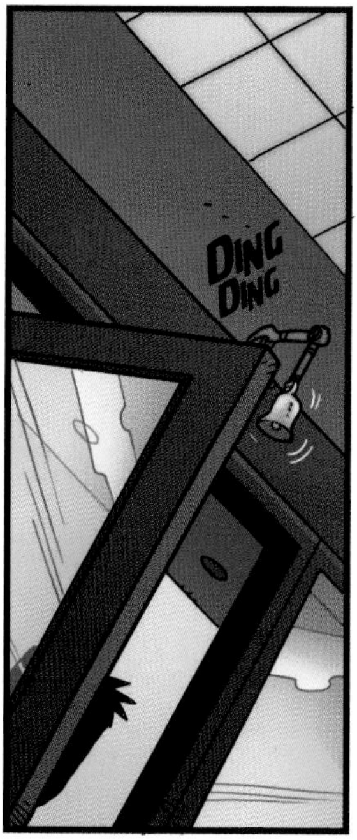
DING
DING

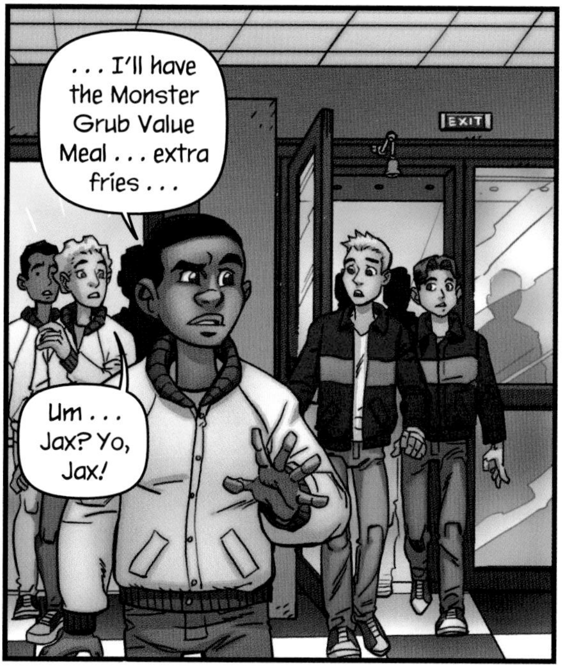
. . . I'll have the Monster Grub Value Meal . . . extra fries . . .
EXIT
Um . . . Jax? Yo, Jax!

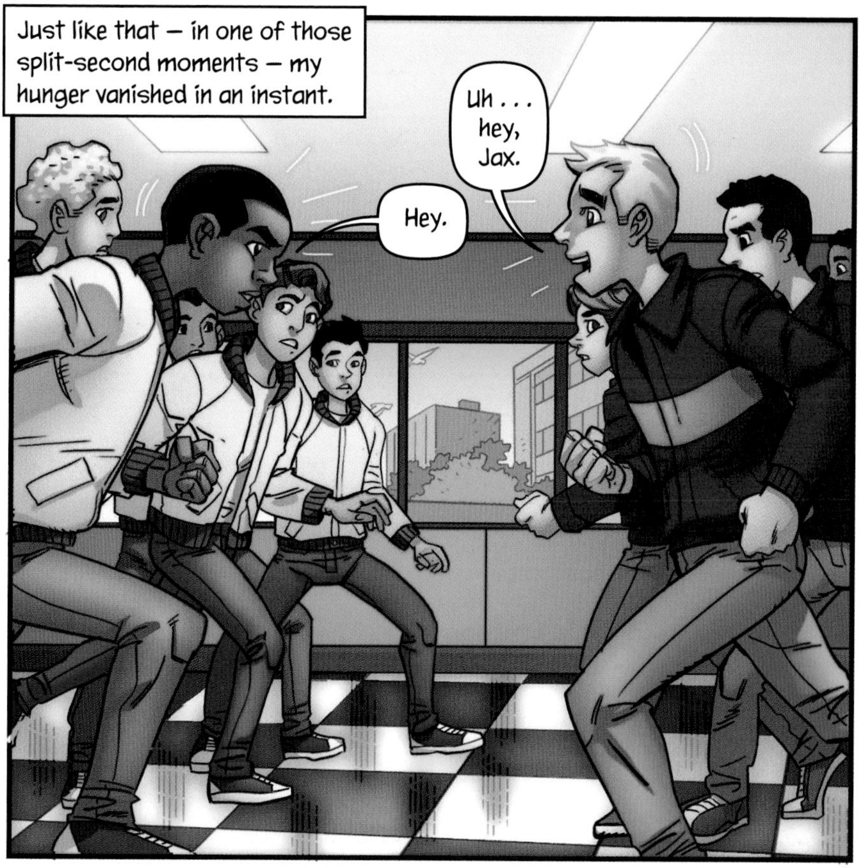
Just like that — in one of those split-second moments — my hunger vanished in an instant.
Uh . . . hey, Jax.
Hey.

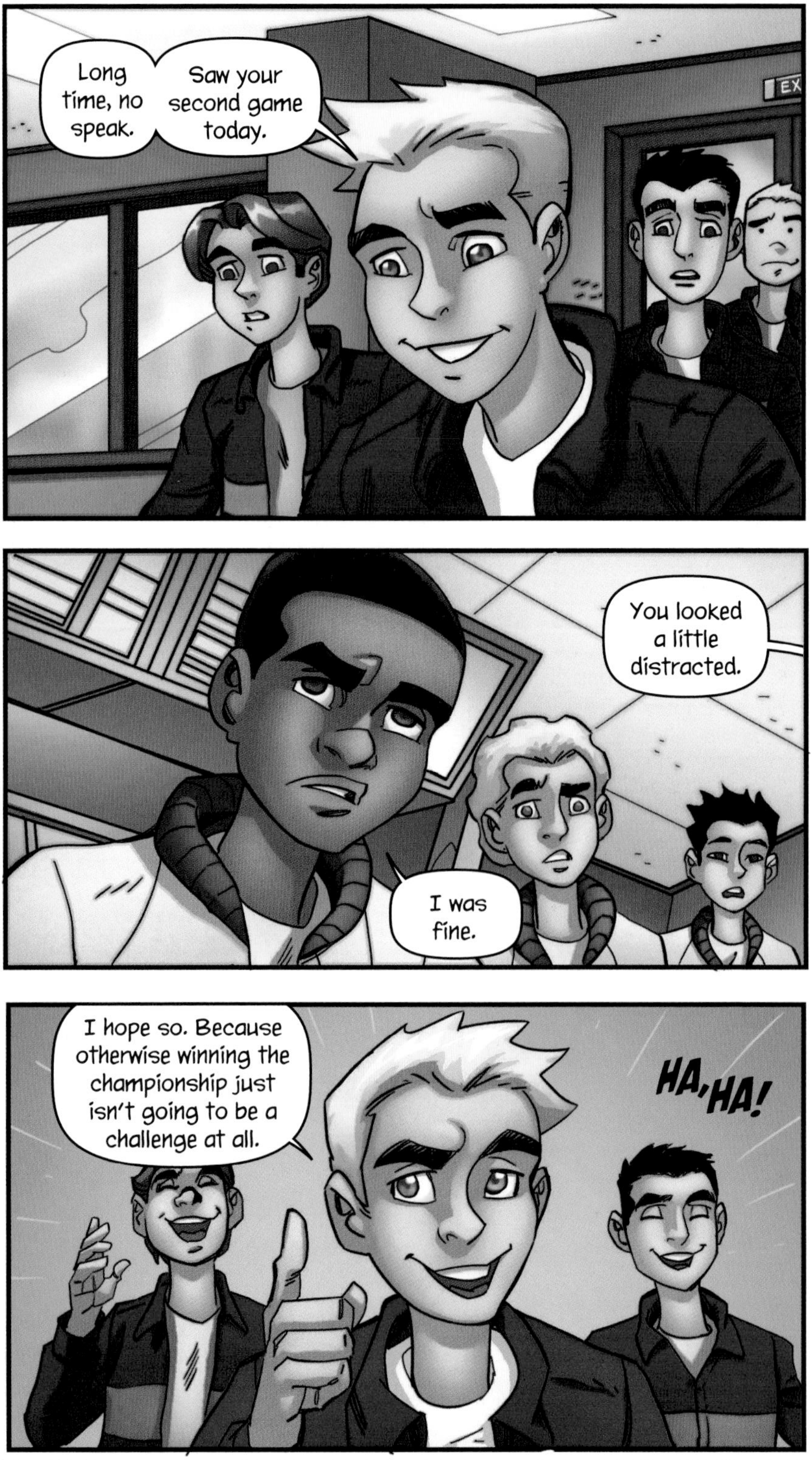
Long time, no speak.
Saw your second game today.
You looked a little distracted.
I was fine.
I hope so. Because otherwise winning the championship just isn't going to be a challenge at all.
HA, HA!

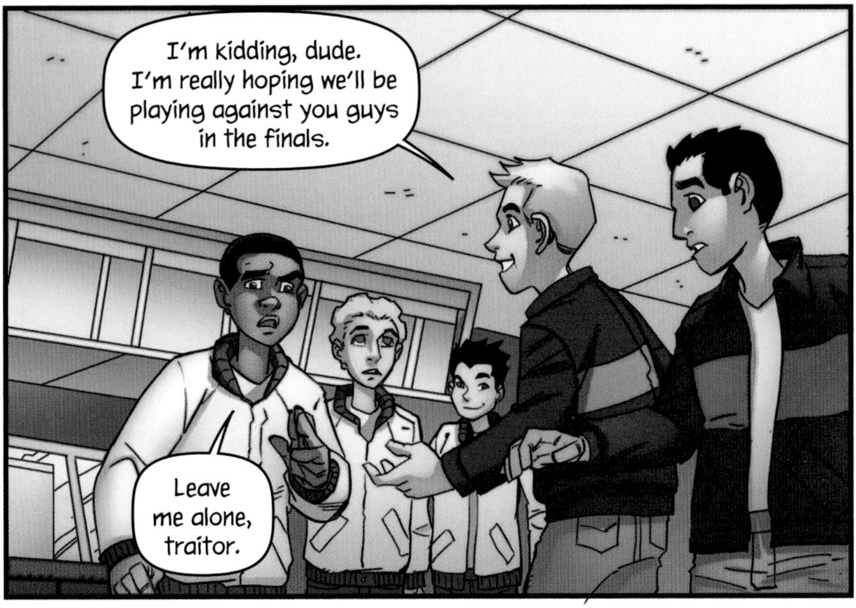
I'm kidding, dude. I'm really hoping we'll be playing against you guys in the finals.
Leave me alone, traitor.

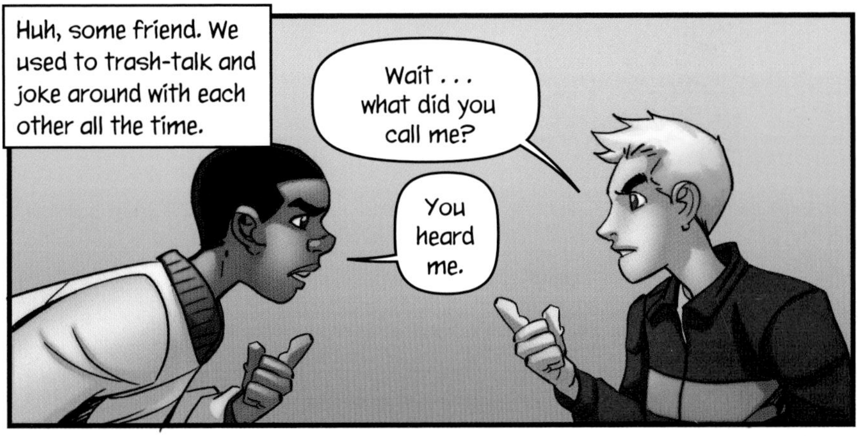
Huh, some friend. We used to trash-talk and joke around with each other all the time.
Wait . . . what did you call me?
You heard me.

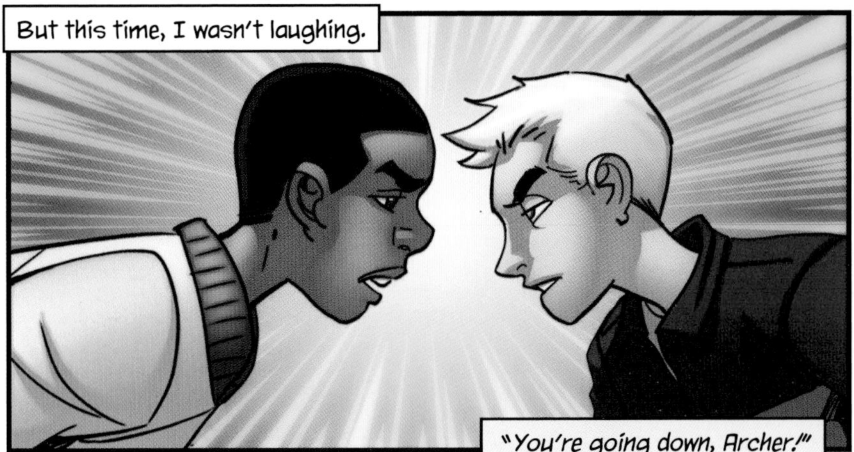
But this time, I wasn't laughing.
"You're going down, Archer!"

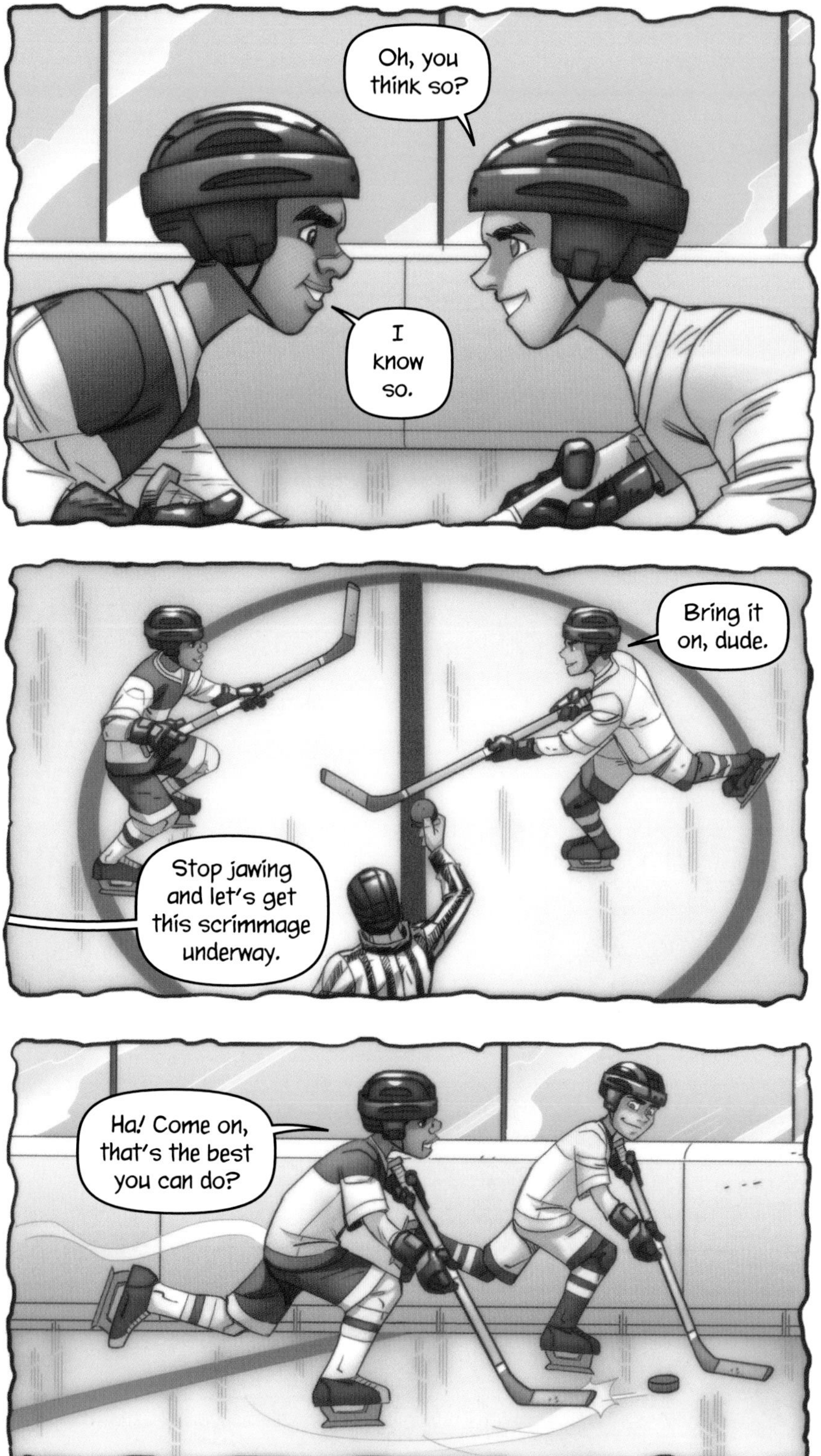
Oh, you think so?
I know so.
Bring it on, dude.
Stop jawing and let's get this scrimmage underway.
Ha! Come on, that's the best you can do?

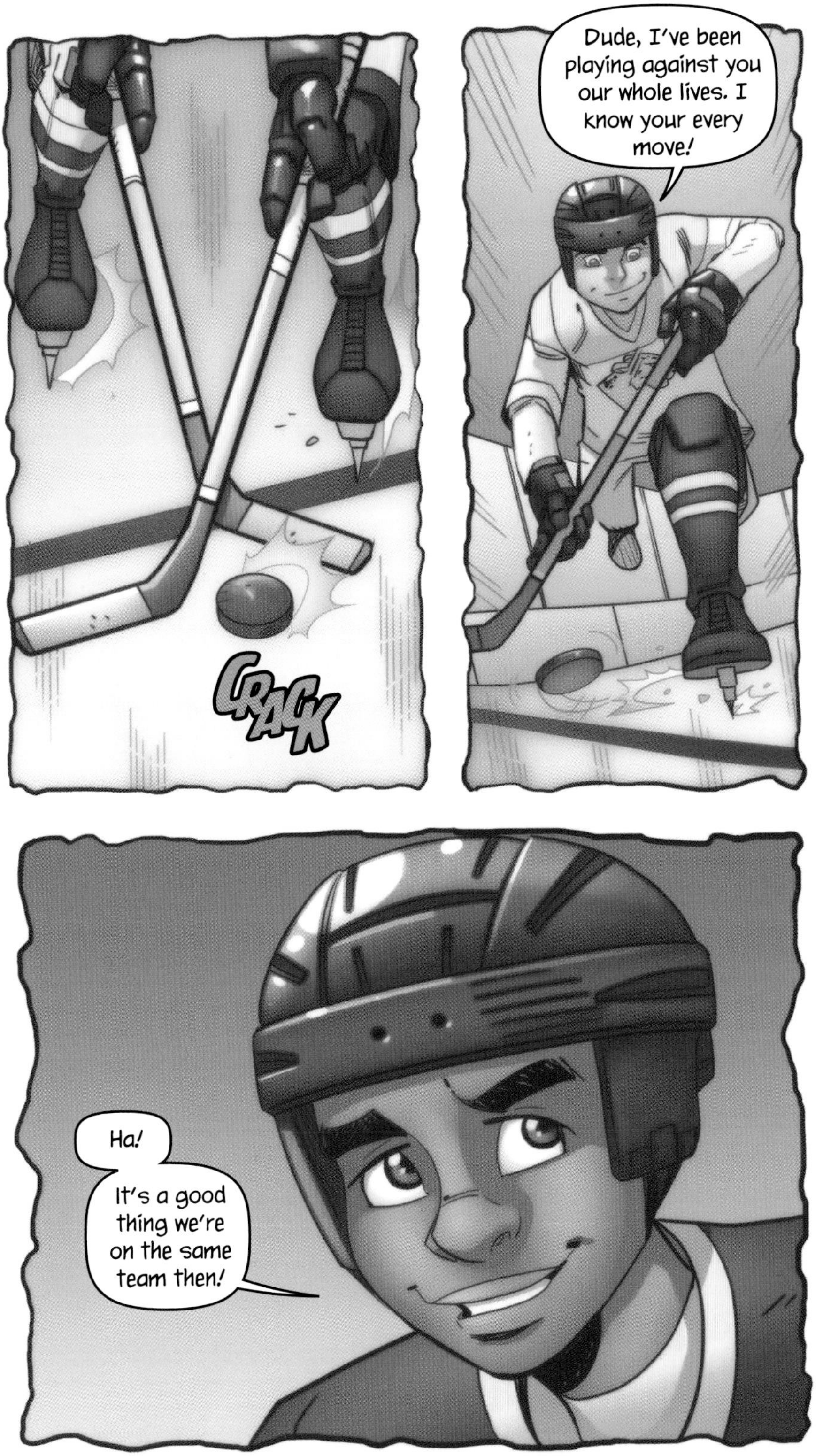
CRACK
Dude, I've been playing against you our whole lives. I know your every move!
Ha!
It's a good thing we're on the same team then!

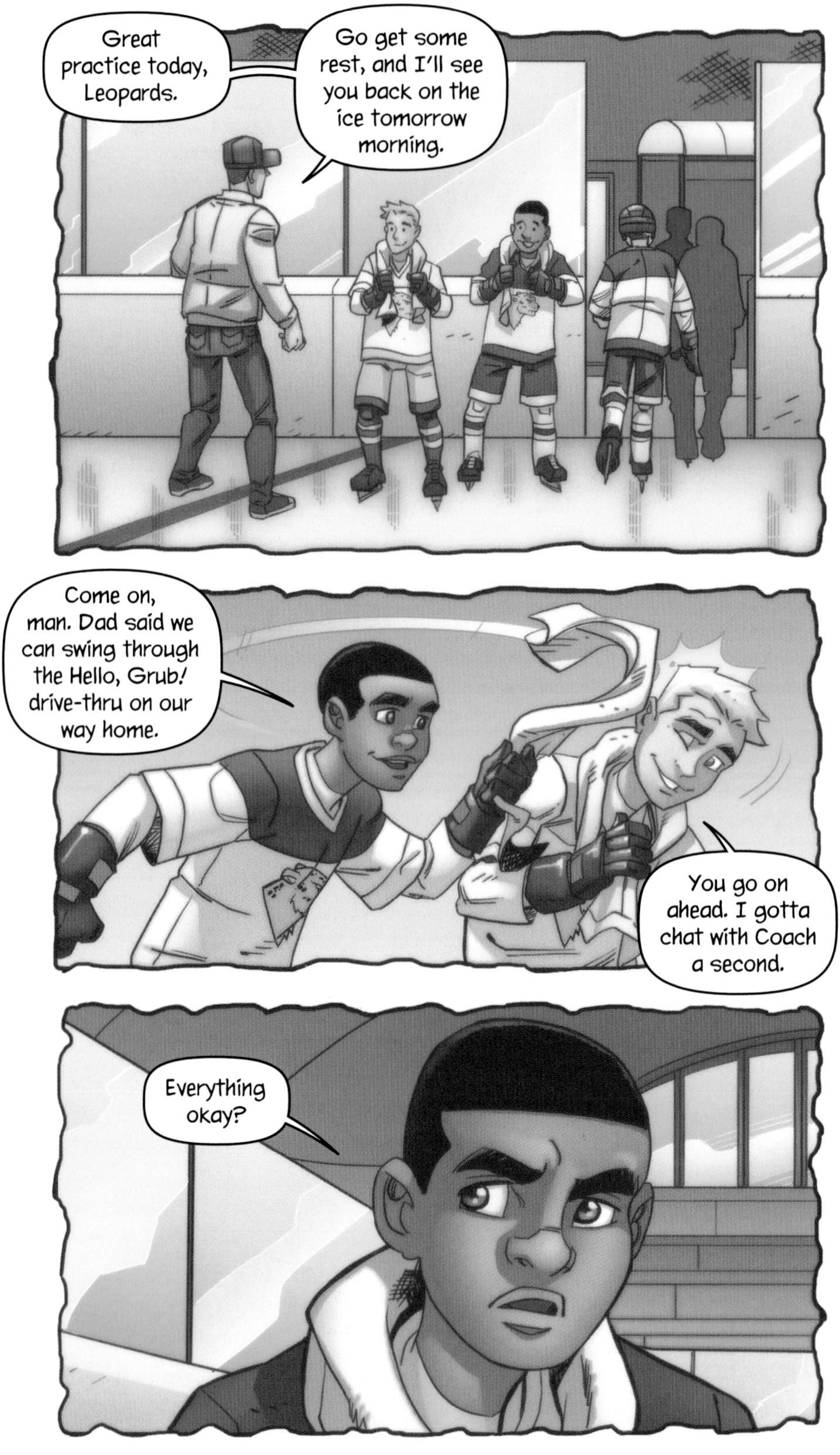
Great practice today, Leopards.
Go get some rest, and I'll see you back on the ice tomorrow morning.
Come on, man. Dad said we can swing through the Hello, Grub! drive-thru on our way home.
You go on ahead. I gotta chat with Coach a second.
Everything okay?

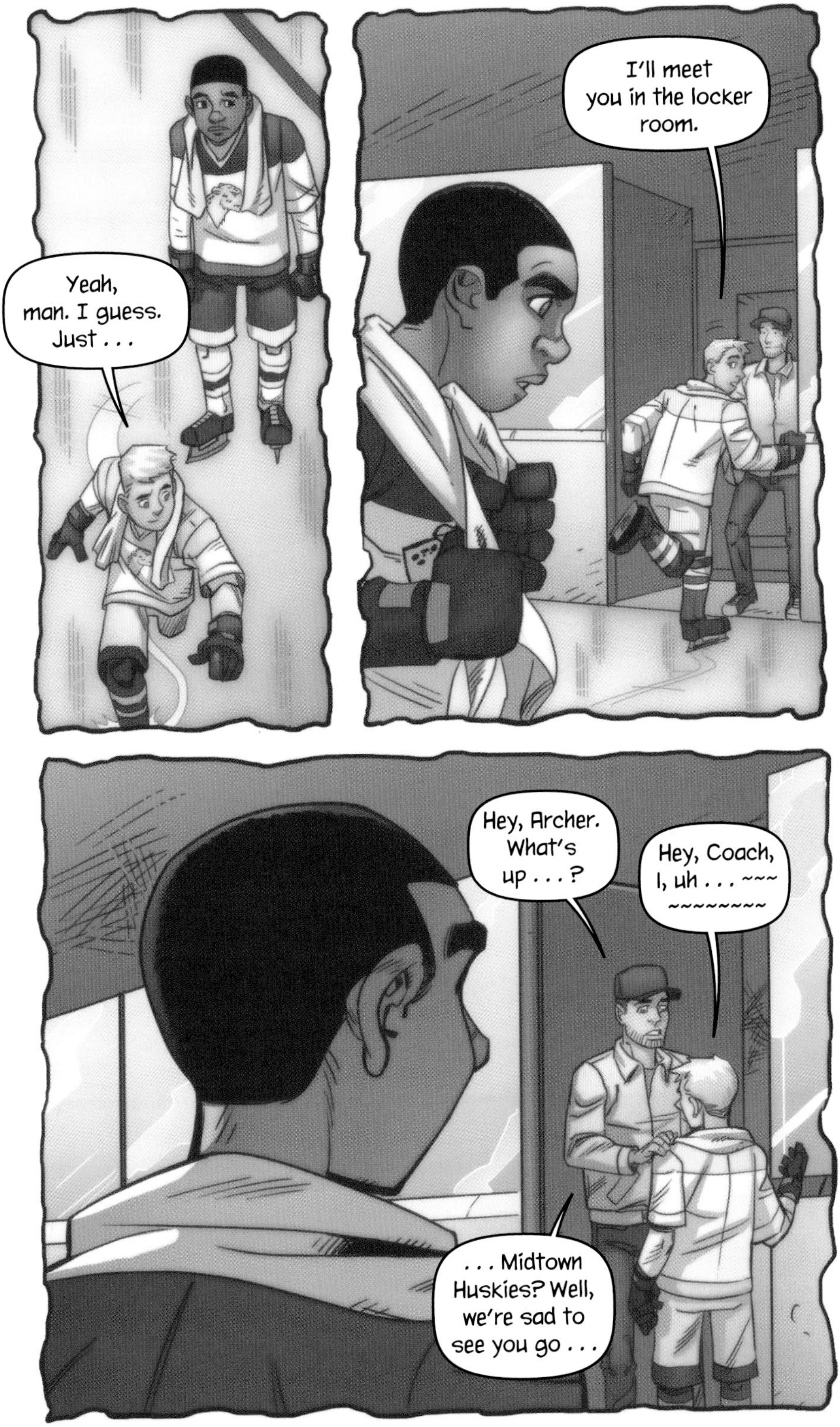
Yeah, man. I guess. Just . . .
I'll meet you in the locker room.
Hey, Archer. What's up . . . ?
Hey, Coach, I, uh . . . ~~~ ~~~~~~~~~
. . . Midtown Huskies? Well, we're sad to see you go . . .

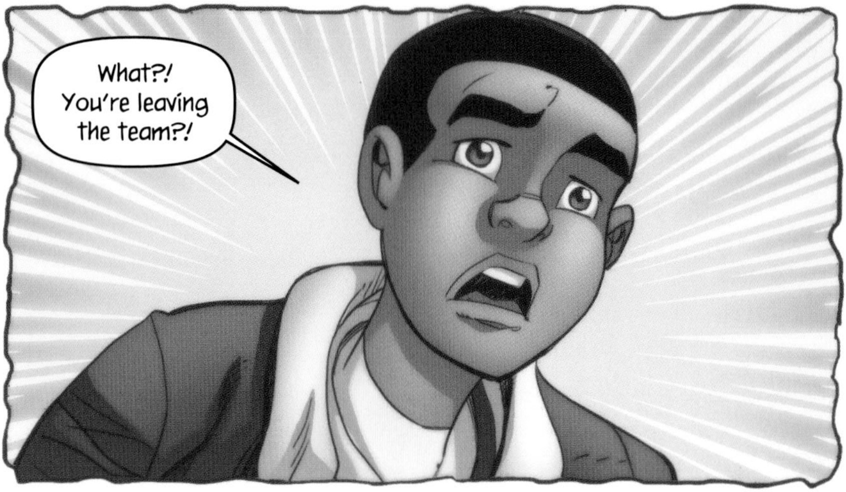
What?! You're leaving the team?!

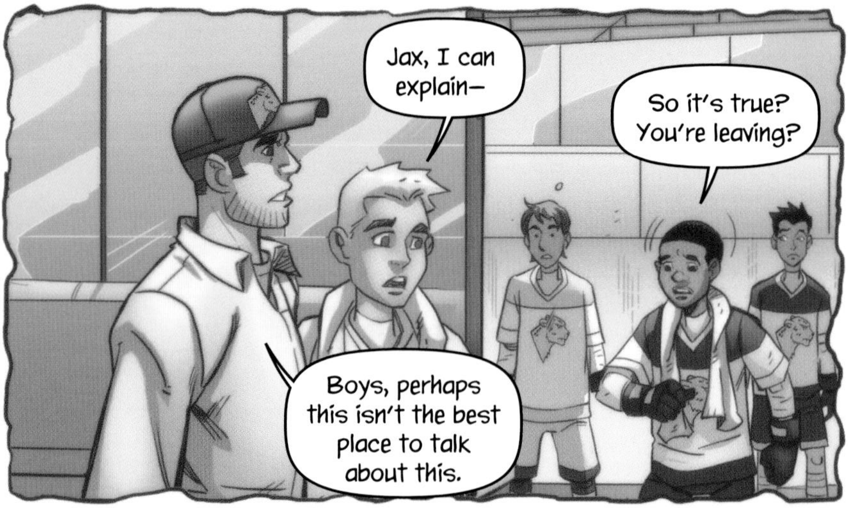
Jax, I can explain–
So it's true? You're leaving?
Boys, perhaps this isn't the best place to talk about this.

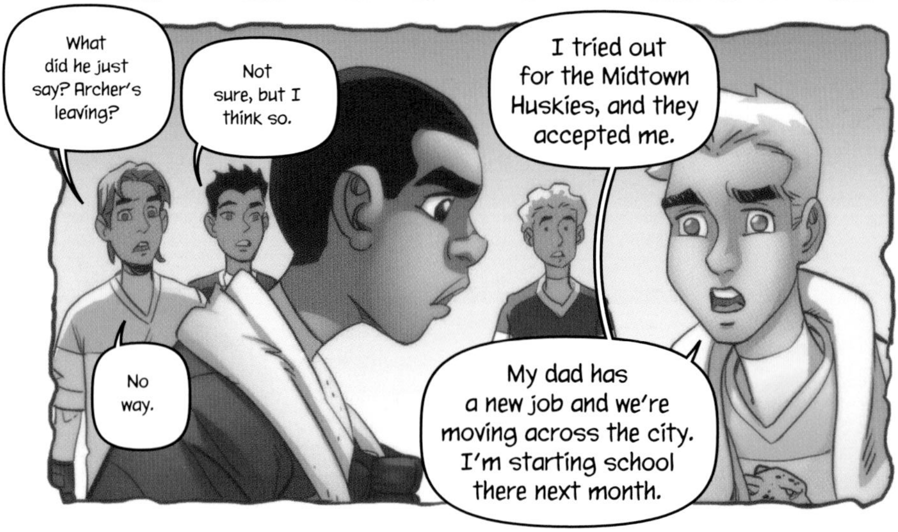
What did he just say? Archer's leaving?
Not sure, but I think so.
No way.
I tried out for the Midtown Huskies, and they accepted me.
My dad has a new job and we're moving across the city. I'm starting school there next month.

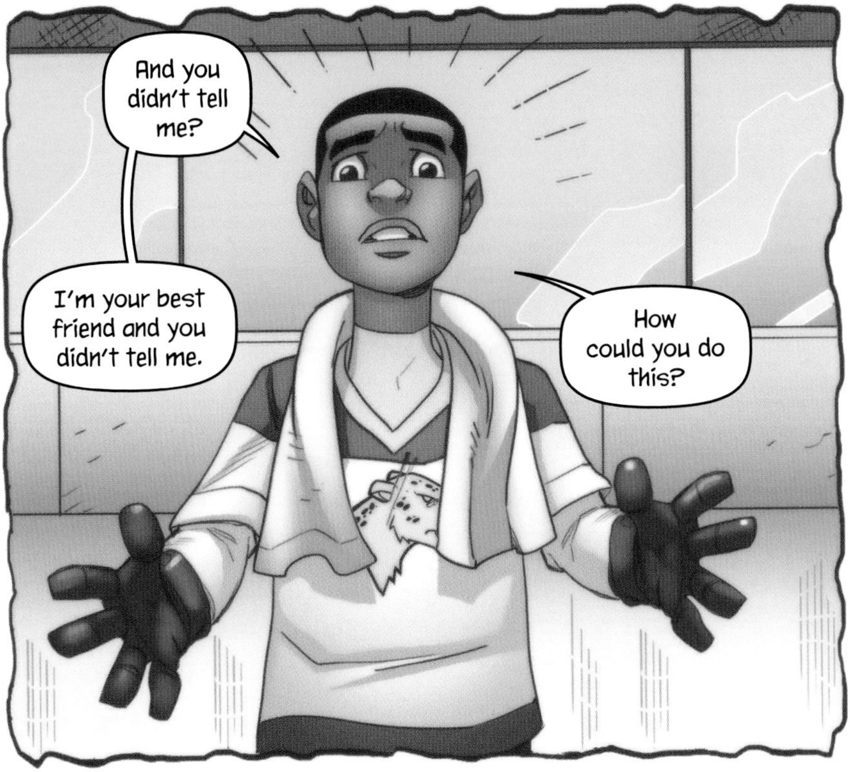
And you didn't tell me?
I'm your best friend and you didn't tell me.
How could you do this?

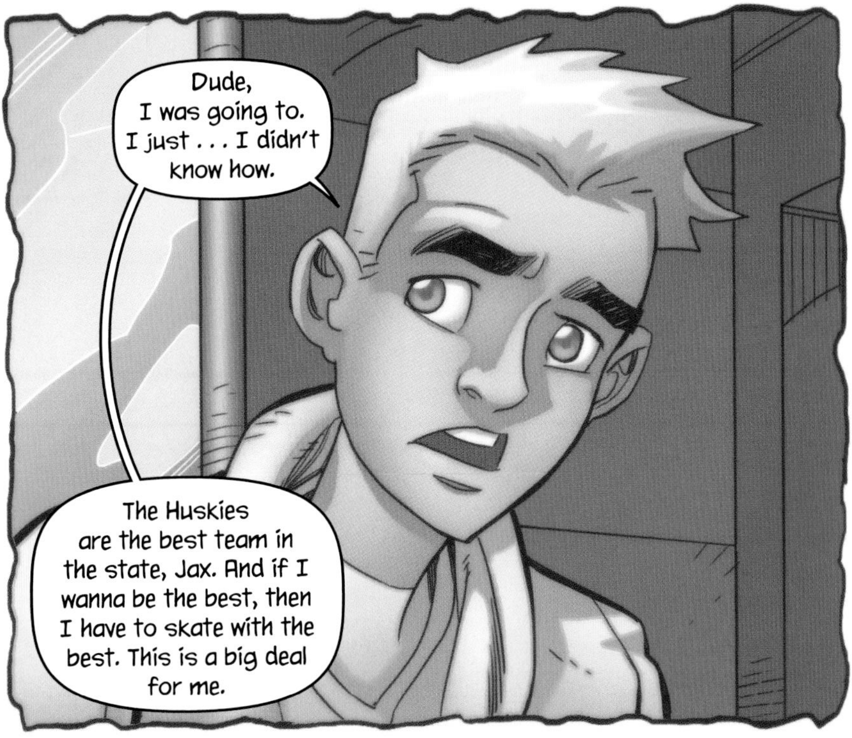
Dude, I was going to. I just . . . I didn't know how.
The Huskies are the best team in the state, Jax. And if I wanna be the best, then I have to skate with the best. This is a big deal for me.

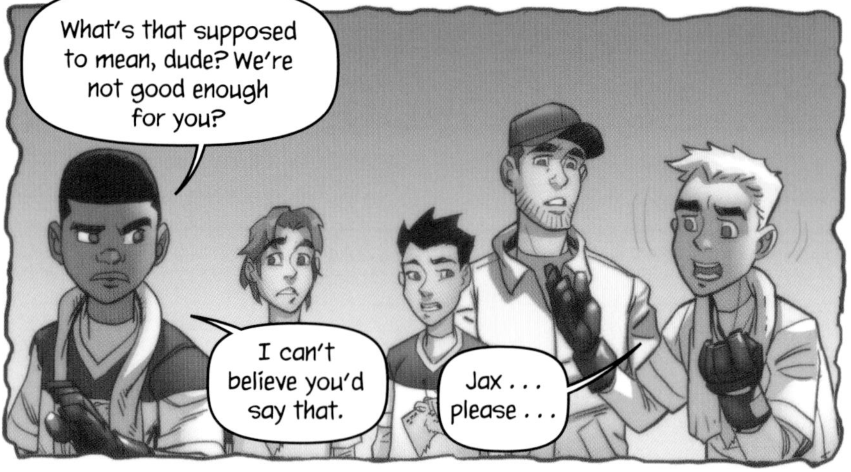
What's that supposed to mean, dude? We're not good enough for you?
I can't believe you'd say that.
Jax . . . please . . .

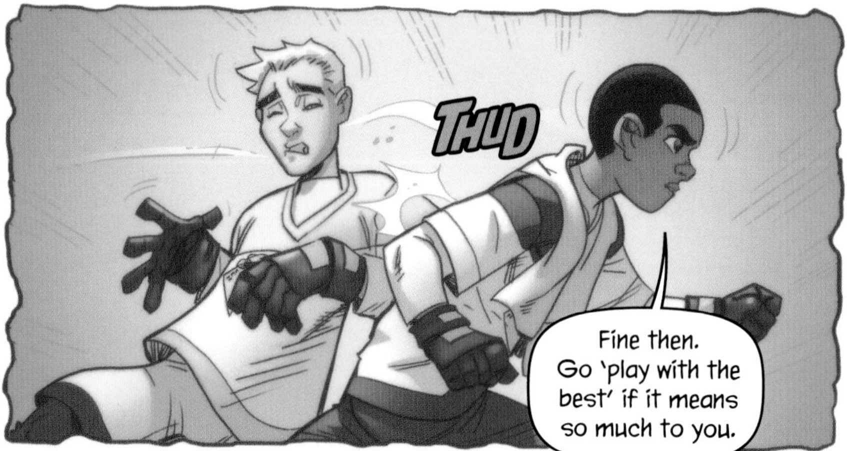
THUD
Fine then. Go 'play with the best' if it means so much to you.

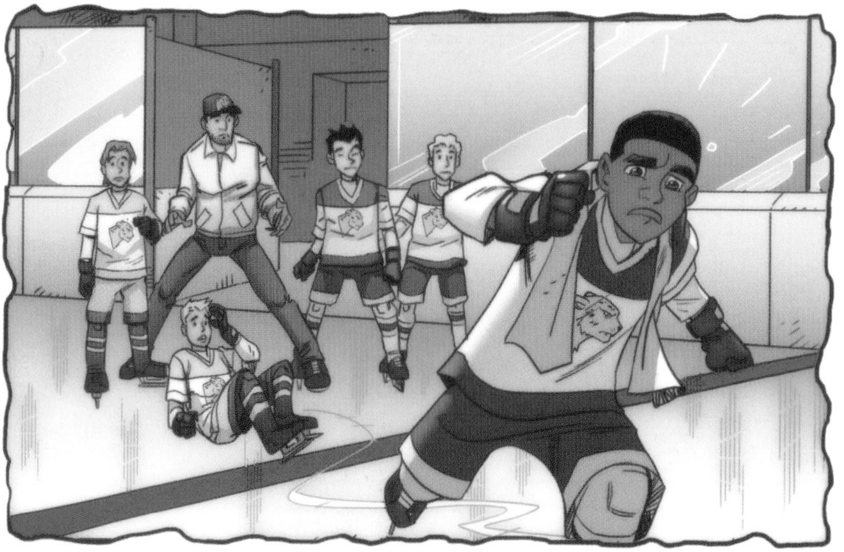

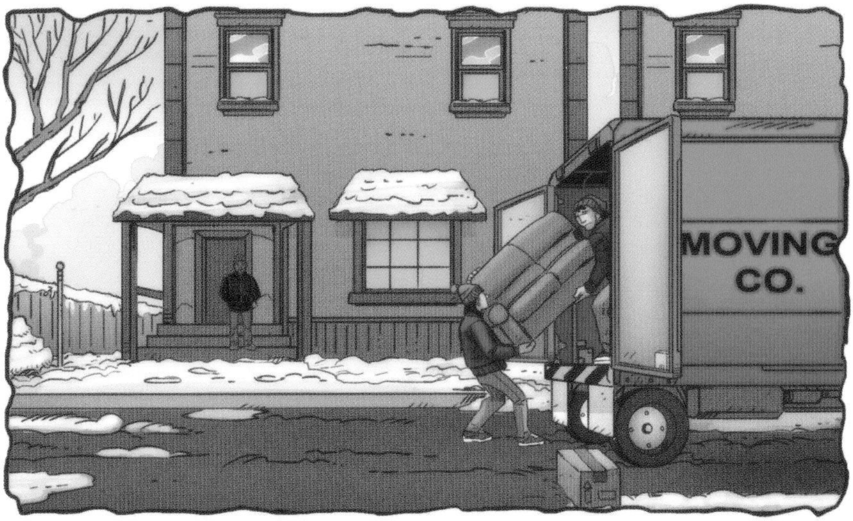
MOVING CO.

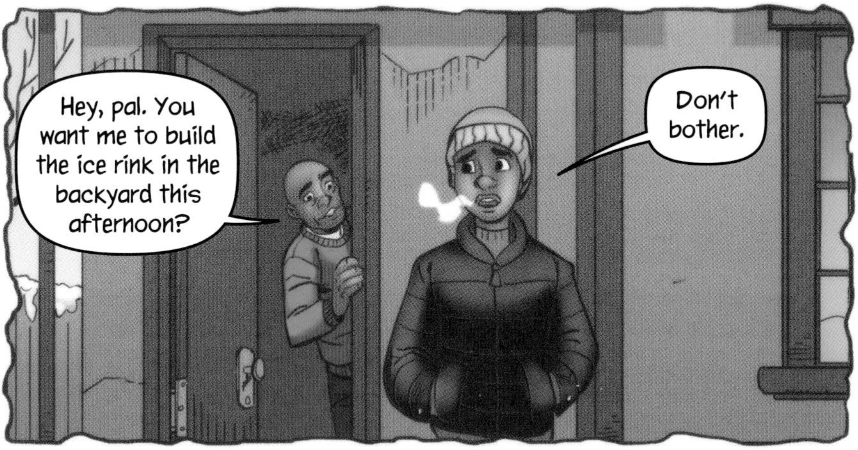
Hey, pal. You want me to build the ice rink in the backyard this afternoon?
Don't bother.

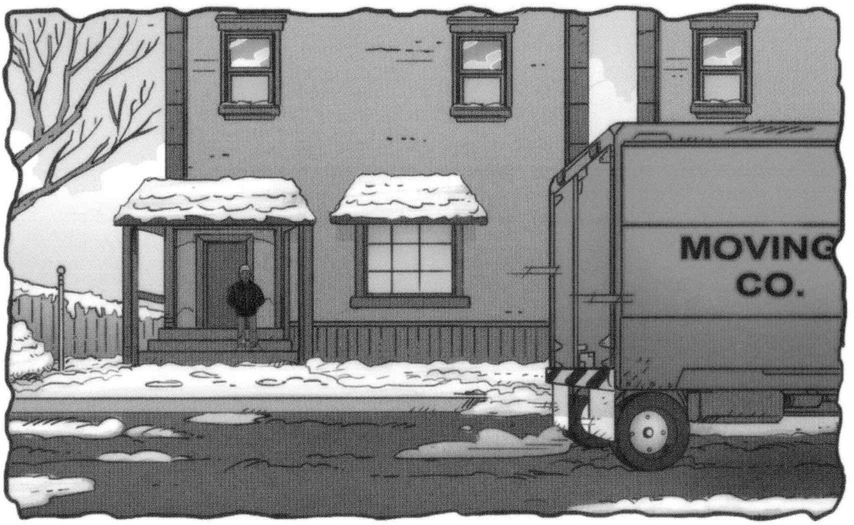
MOVING CO.

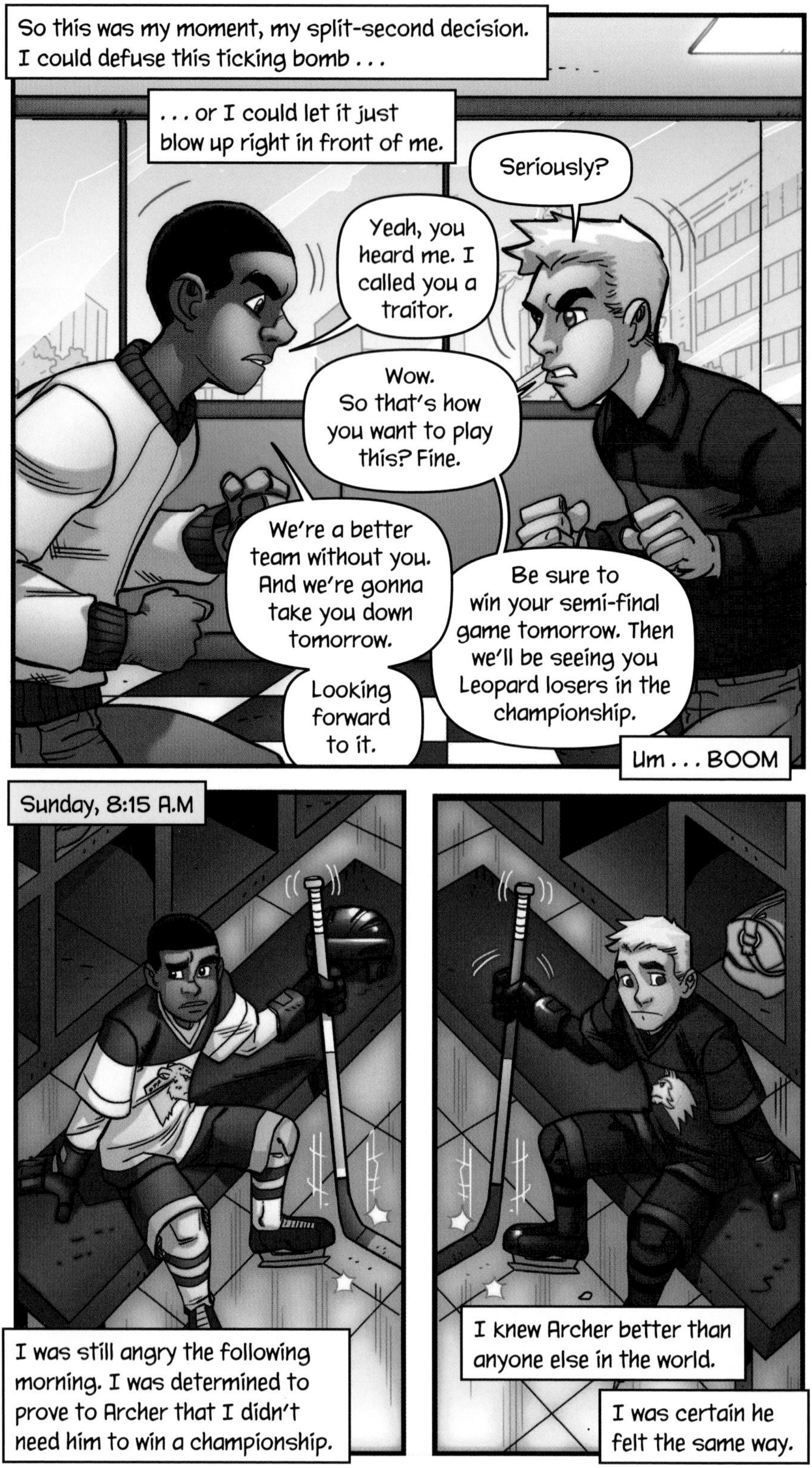

So this was my moment, my split-second decision. I could defuse this ticking bomb . . .
. . . or I could let it just blow up right in front of me.
Seriously?
Yeah, you heard me. I called you a traitor.
Wow. So that's how you want to play this? Fine.
We're a better team without you. And we're gonna take you down tomorrow.
Be sure to win your semi-final game tomorrow. Then we'll be seeing you Leopard losers in the championship.
Looking forward to it.
Um . . . BOOM
Sunday, 8:15 A.M
I was still angry the following morning. I was determined to prove to Archer that I didn't need him to win a championship.
I knew Archer better than anyone else in the world.
I was certain he felt the same way.

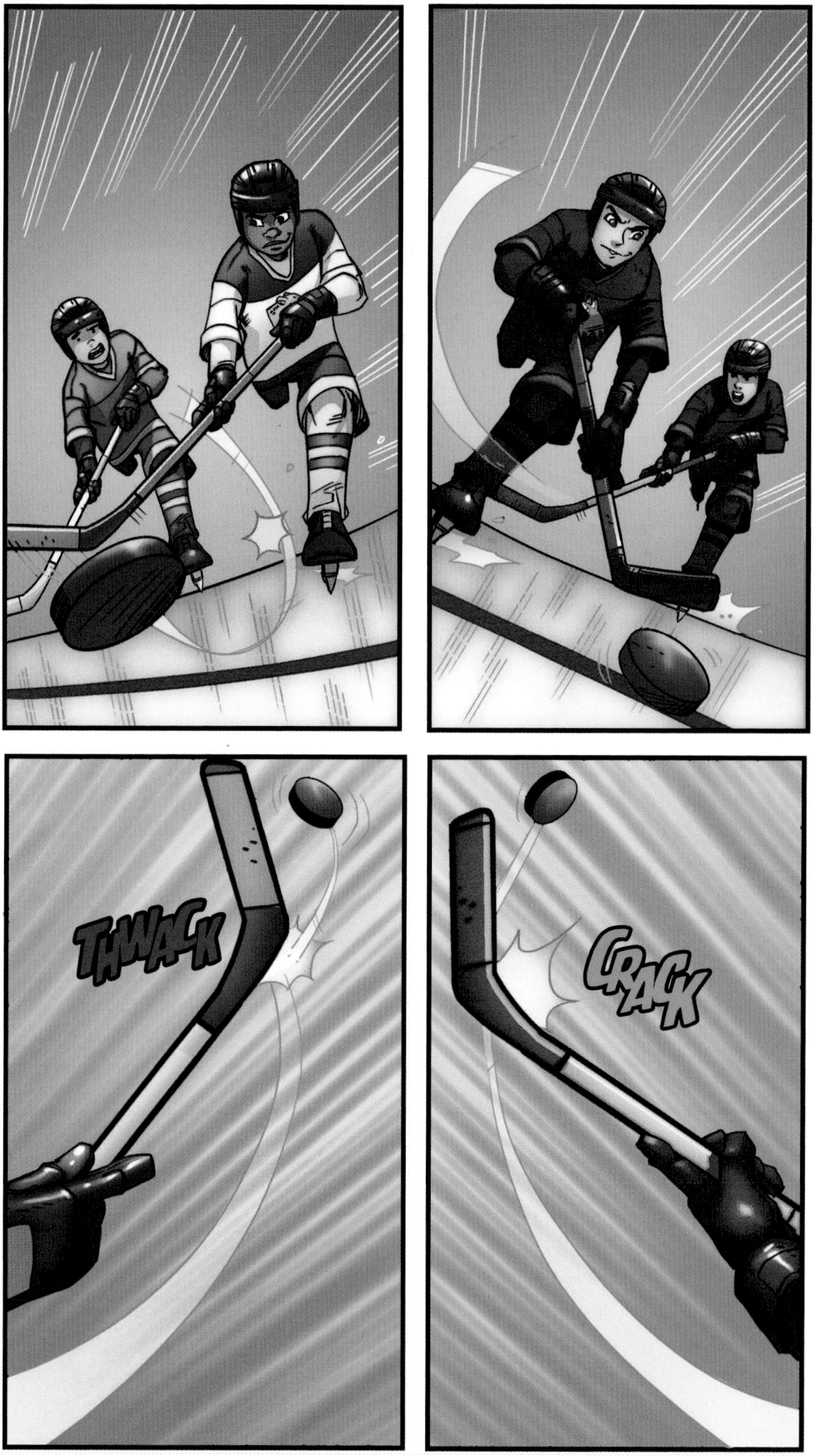
THWACK
CRACK

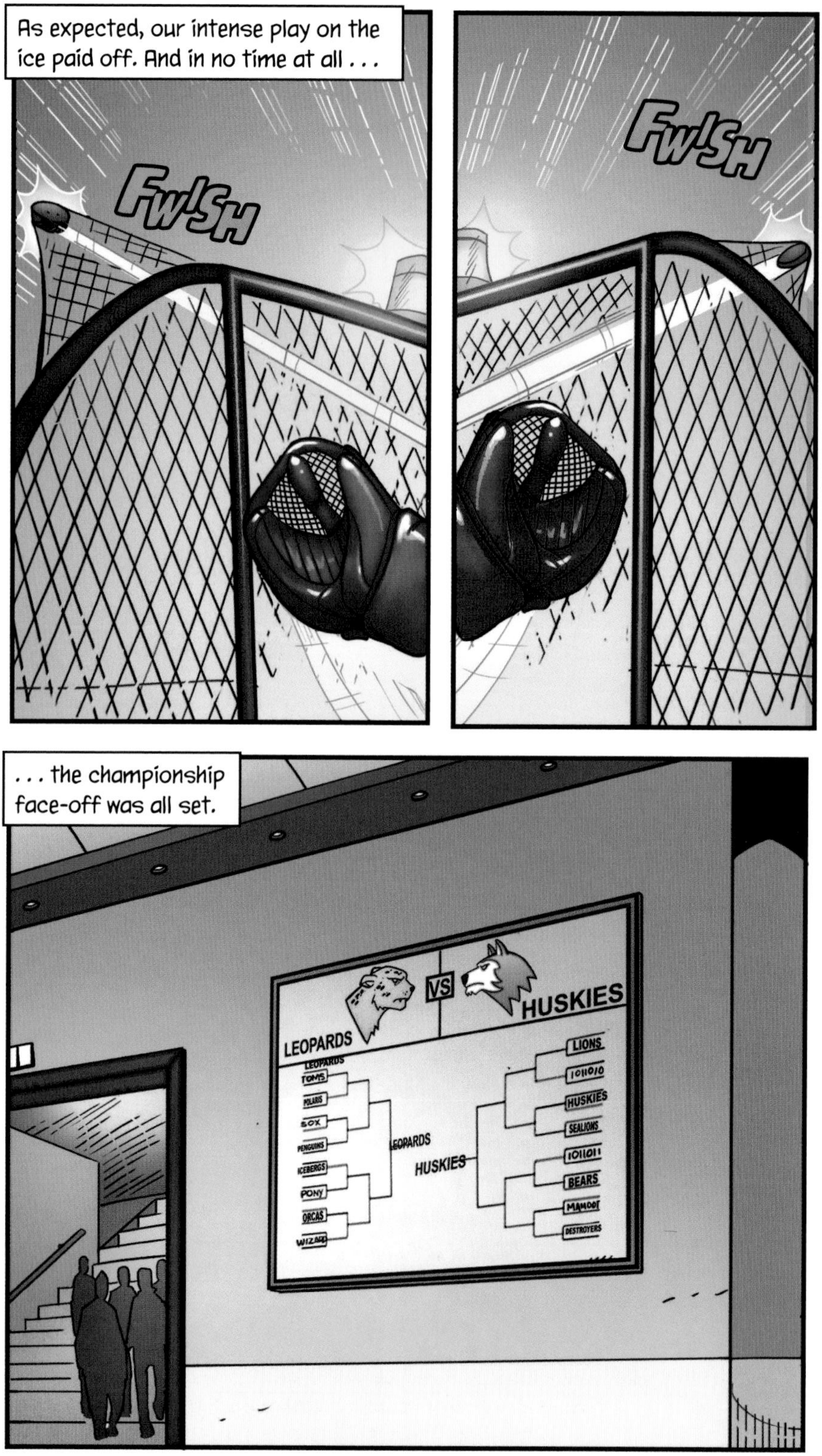
As expected, our intense play on the ice paid off. And in no time at all . . .
FW!SH
FW!SH
. . . the championship face-off was all set.
LEOPARDS
VS
HUSKIES
LIONS
HUSKIES
BEARS
LEOPARDS
HUSKIES

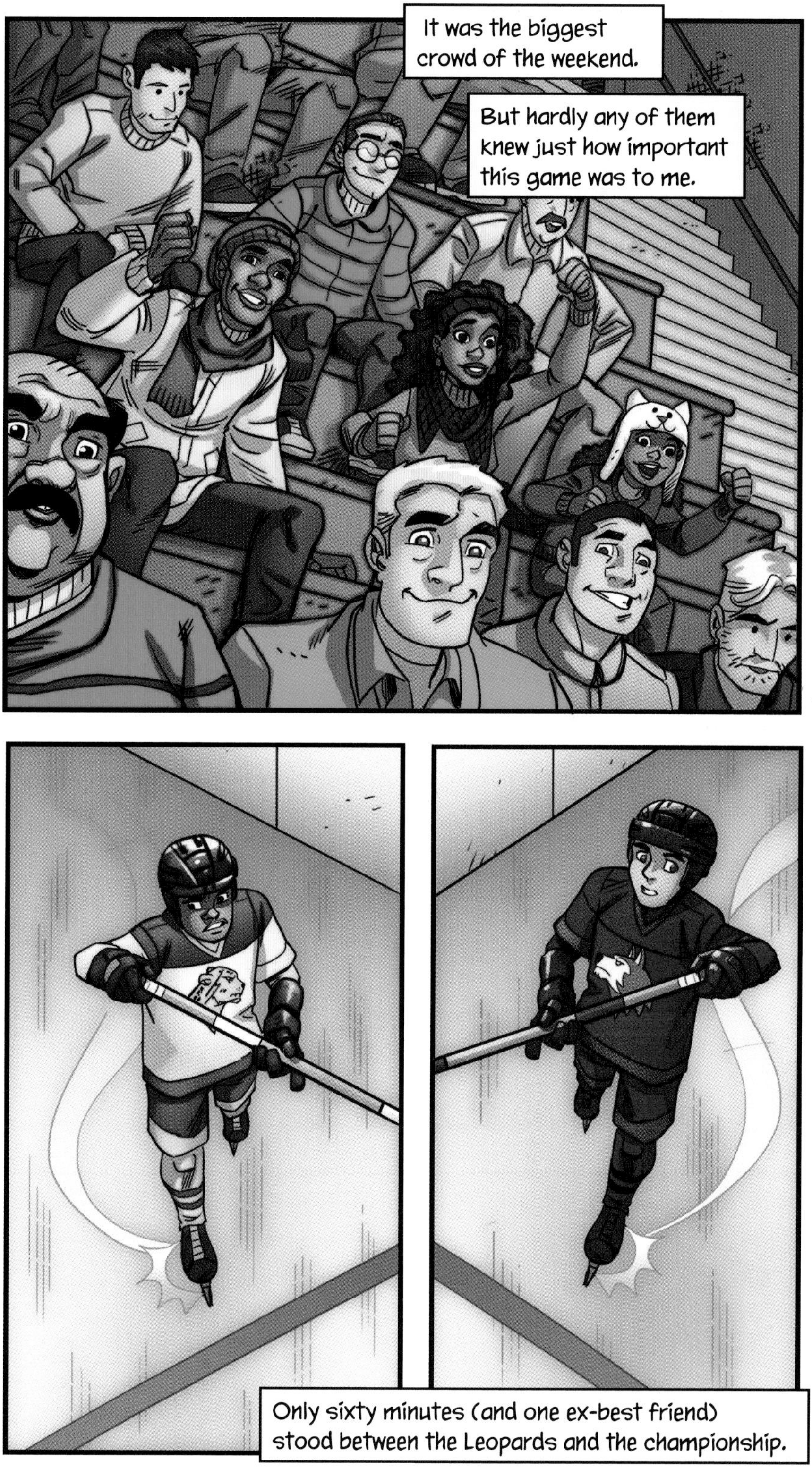
It was the biggest crowd of the weekend.
But hardly any of them knew just how important this game was to me.
Only sixty minutes (and one ex-best friend) stood between the Leopards and the championship.

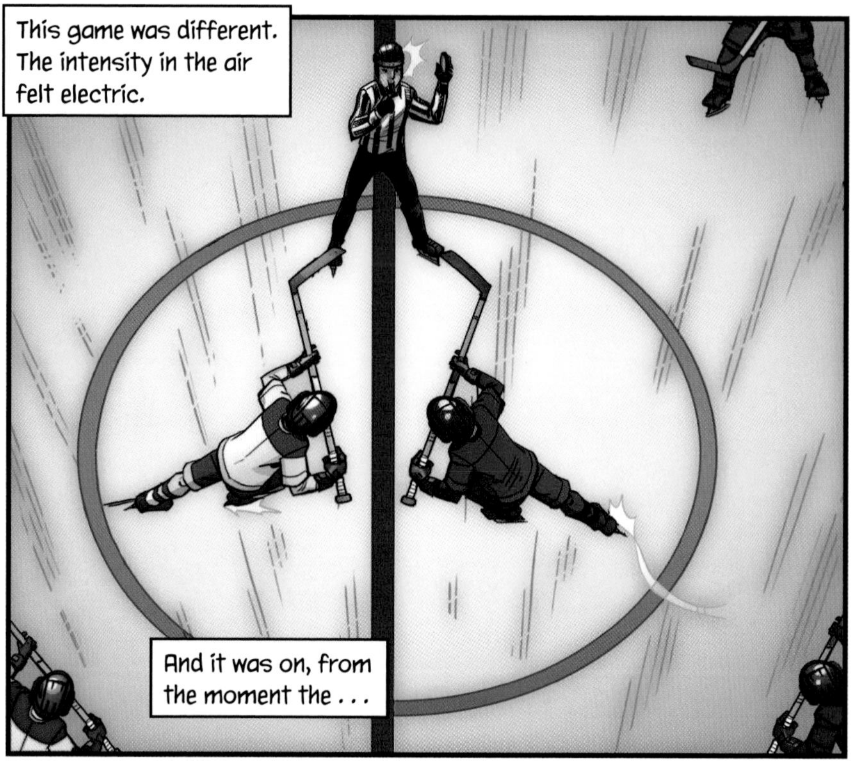
This game was different. The intensity in the air felt electric.
And it was on, from the moment the . . .

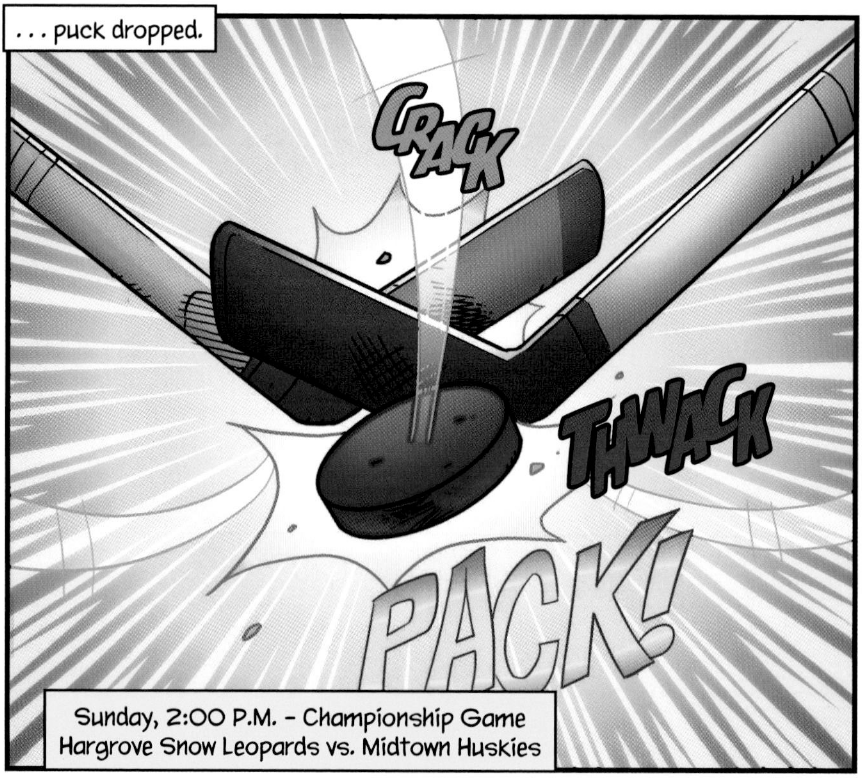
. . . puck dropped.
CRACK
THWACK
PACK!
Sunday, 2:00 P.M. - Championship Game
Hargrove Snow Leopards vs. Midtown Huskies

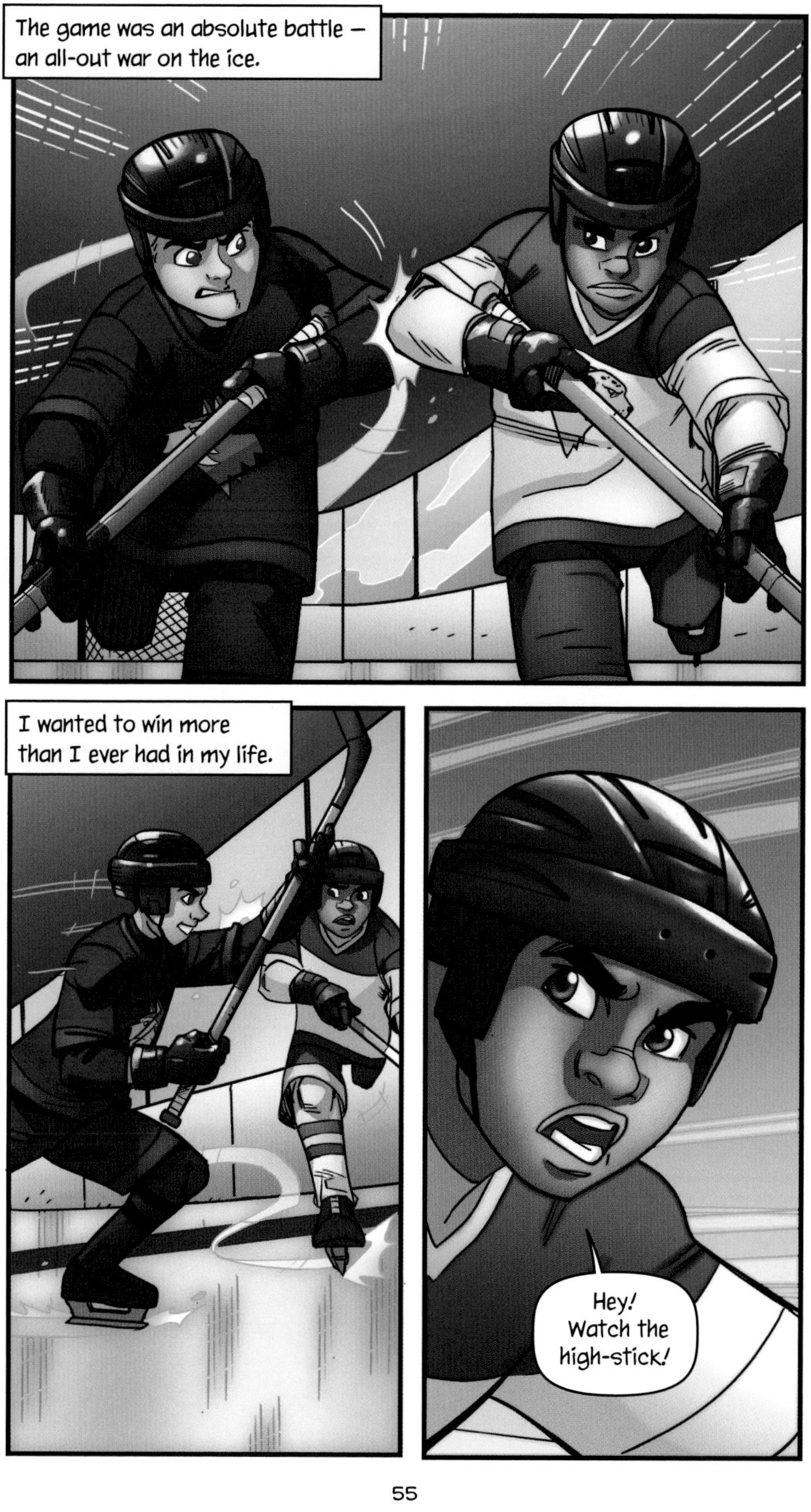
The game was an absolute battle — an all-out war on the ice.
I wanted to win more than I ever had in my life.
Hey! Watch the high-stick!

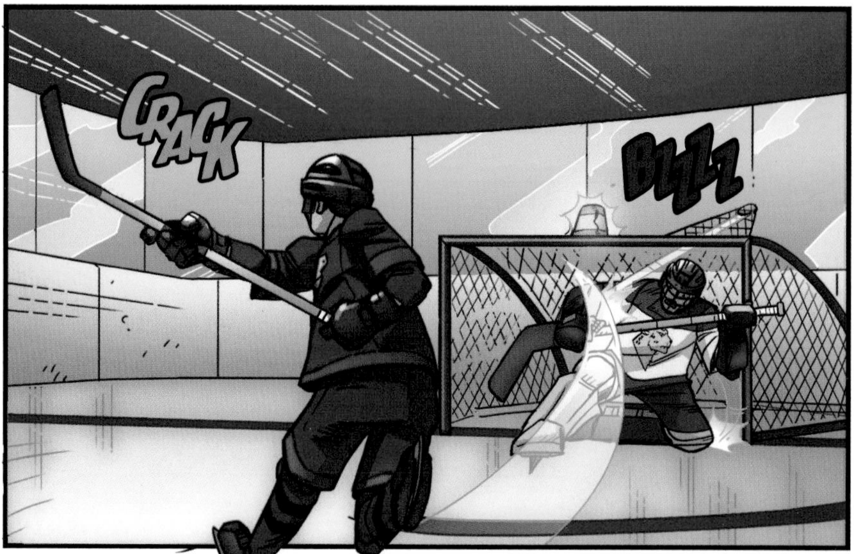
CRACK
BZZZ

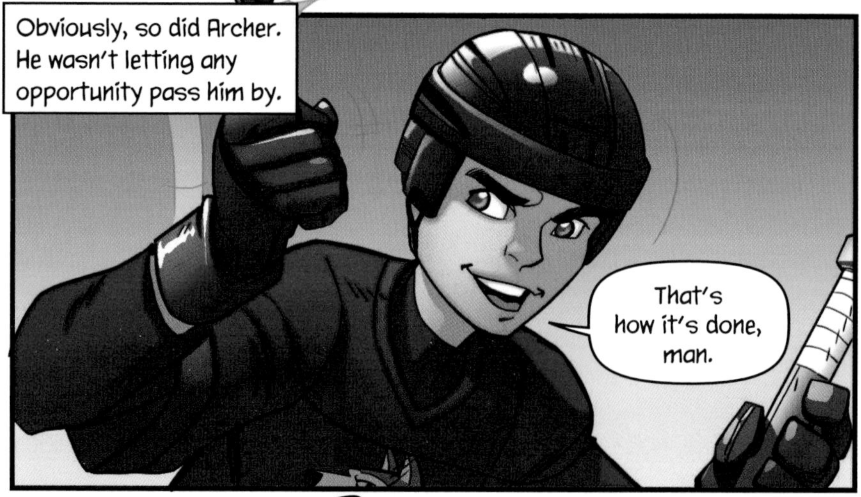
Obviously, so did Archer. He wasn't letting any opportunity pass him by.
That's how it's done, man.

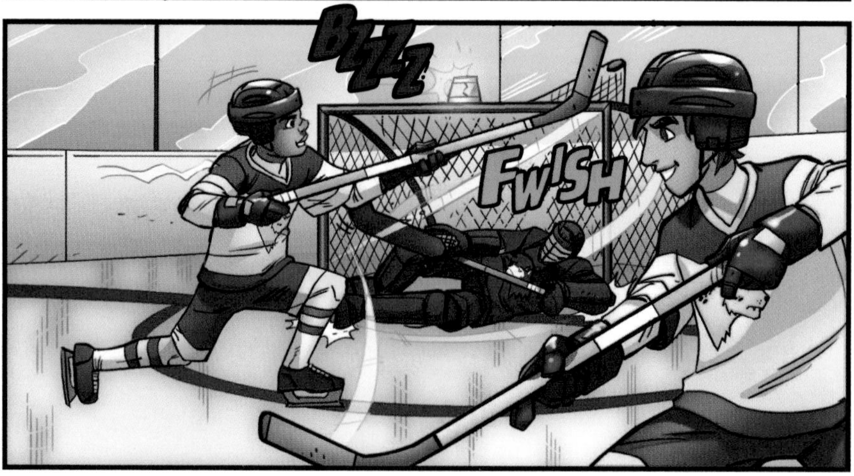
BZZZ
FW!SH

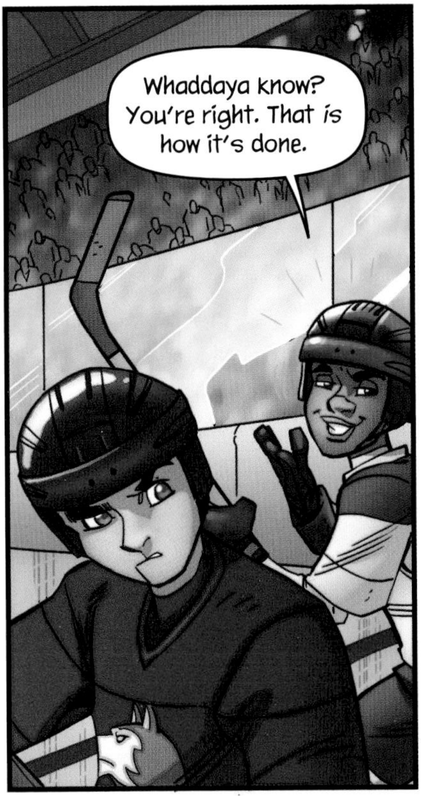
Whaddaya know? You're right. That *is* how it's done.

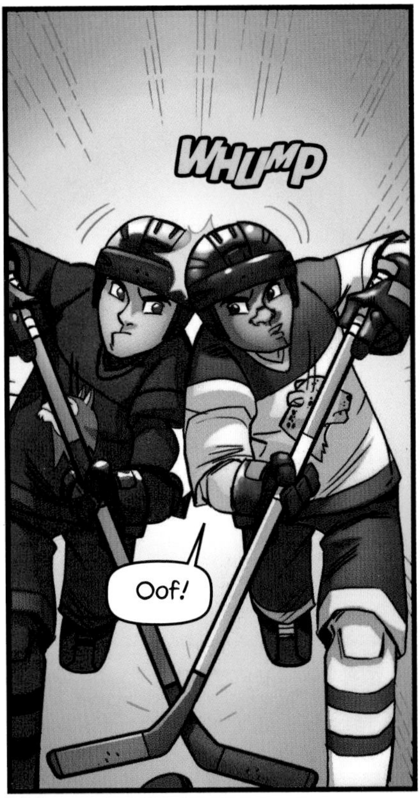
WHUMP
Oof!

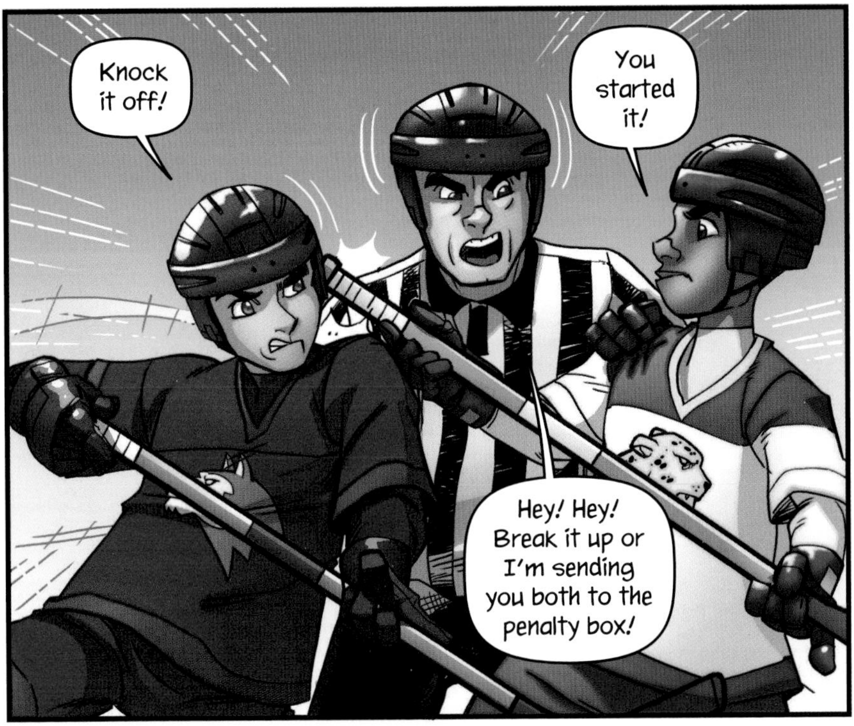
Knock it off!
You started it!
Hey! Hey! Break it up or I'm sending you both to the penalty box!

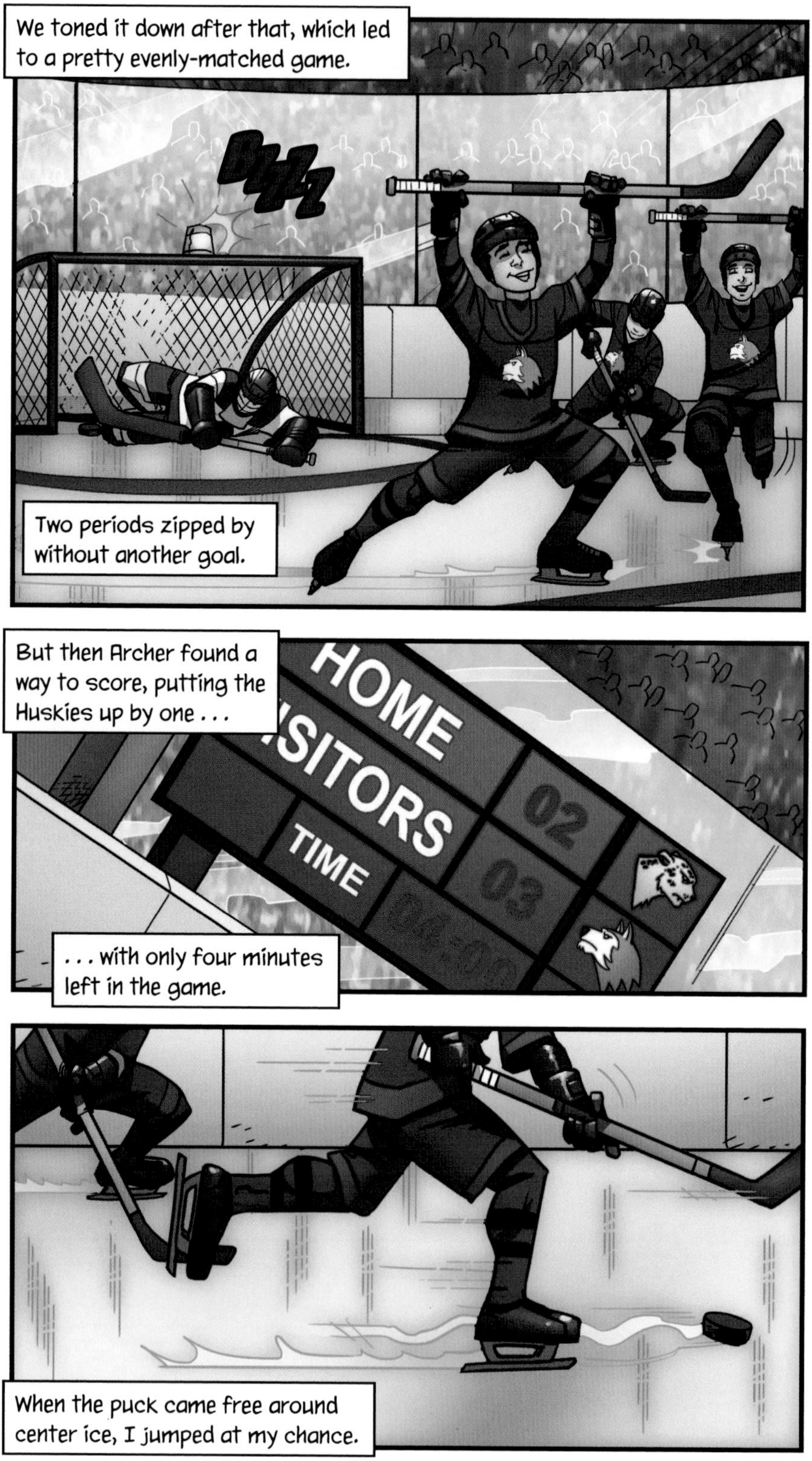
We toned it down after that, which led to a pretty evenly-matched game.
Two periods zipped by without another goal.
But then Archer found a way to score, putting the Huskies up by one . . .
HOME
TIME
02
03
. . . with only four minutes left in the game.
When the puck came free around center ice, I jumped at my chance.

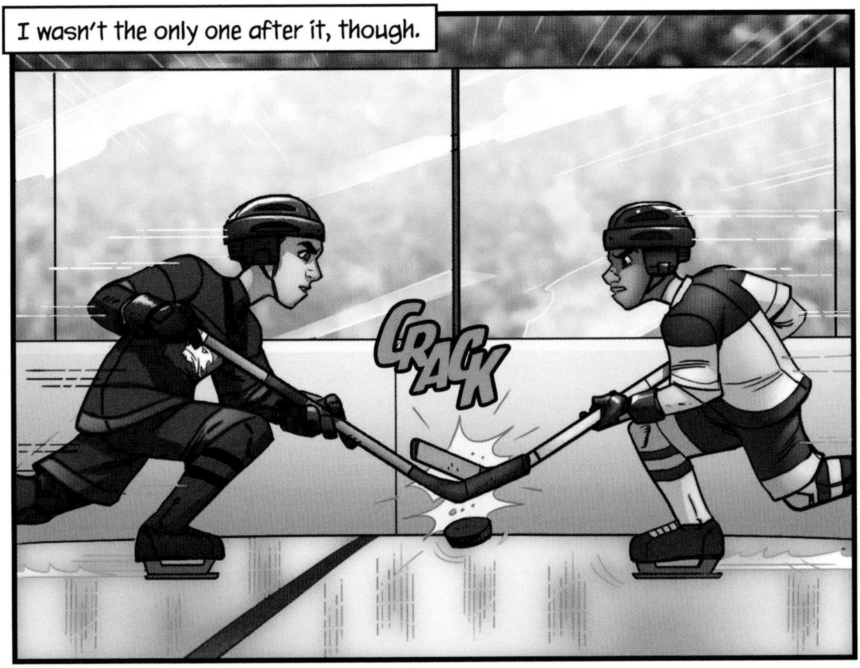
I wasn't the only one after it, though.
CRACK

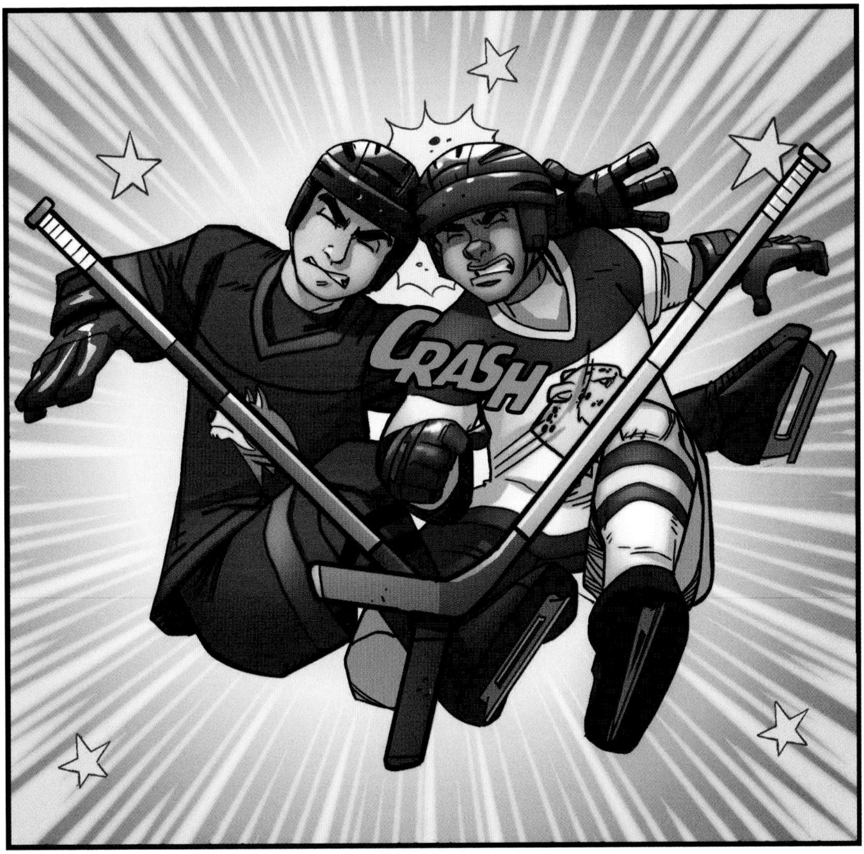
CRASH

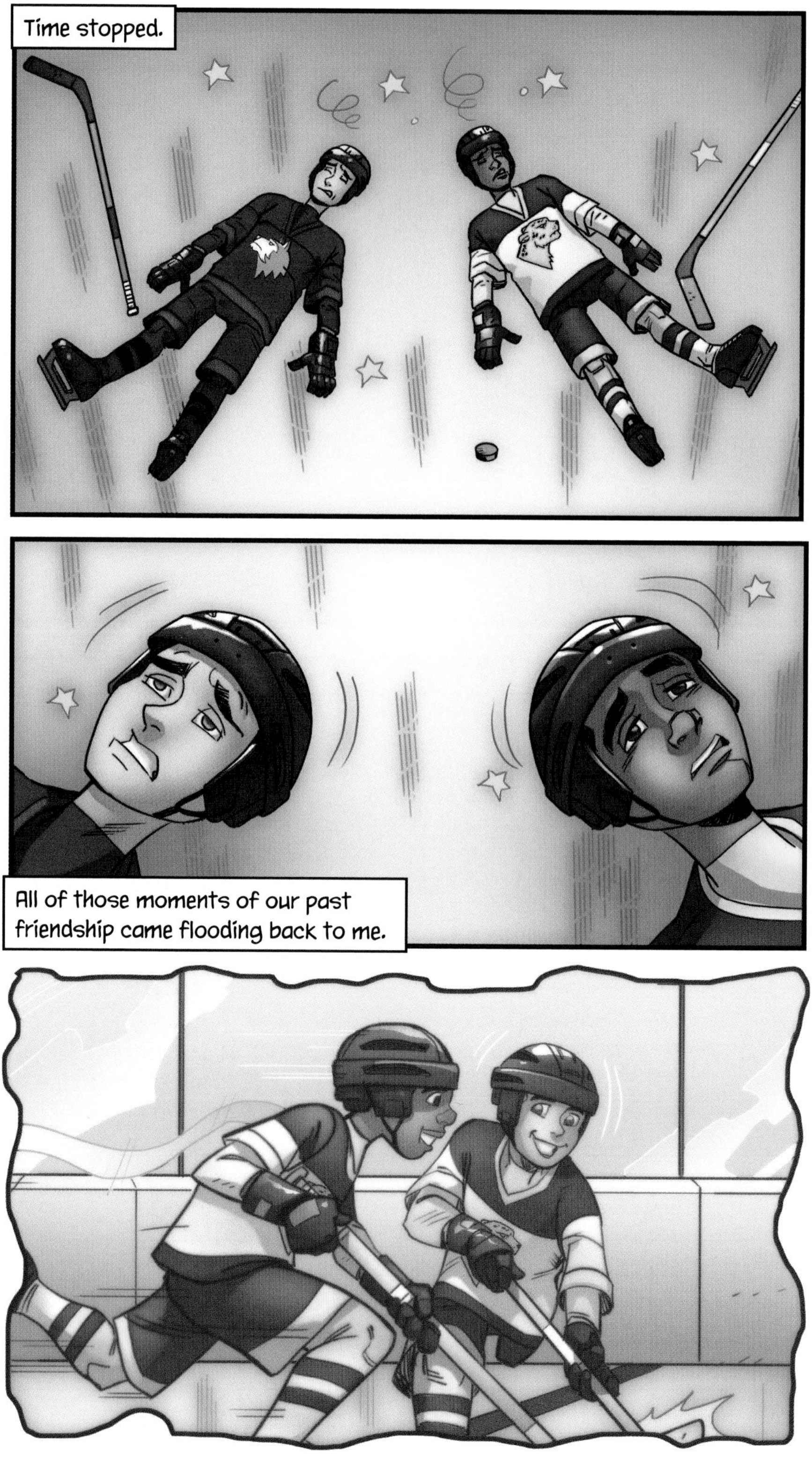
Time stopped.
All of those moments of our past friendship came flooding back to me.

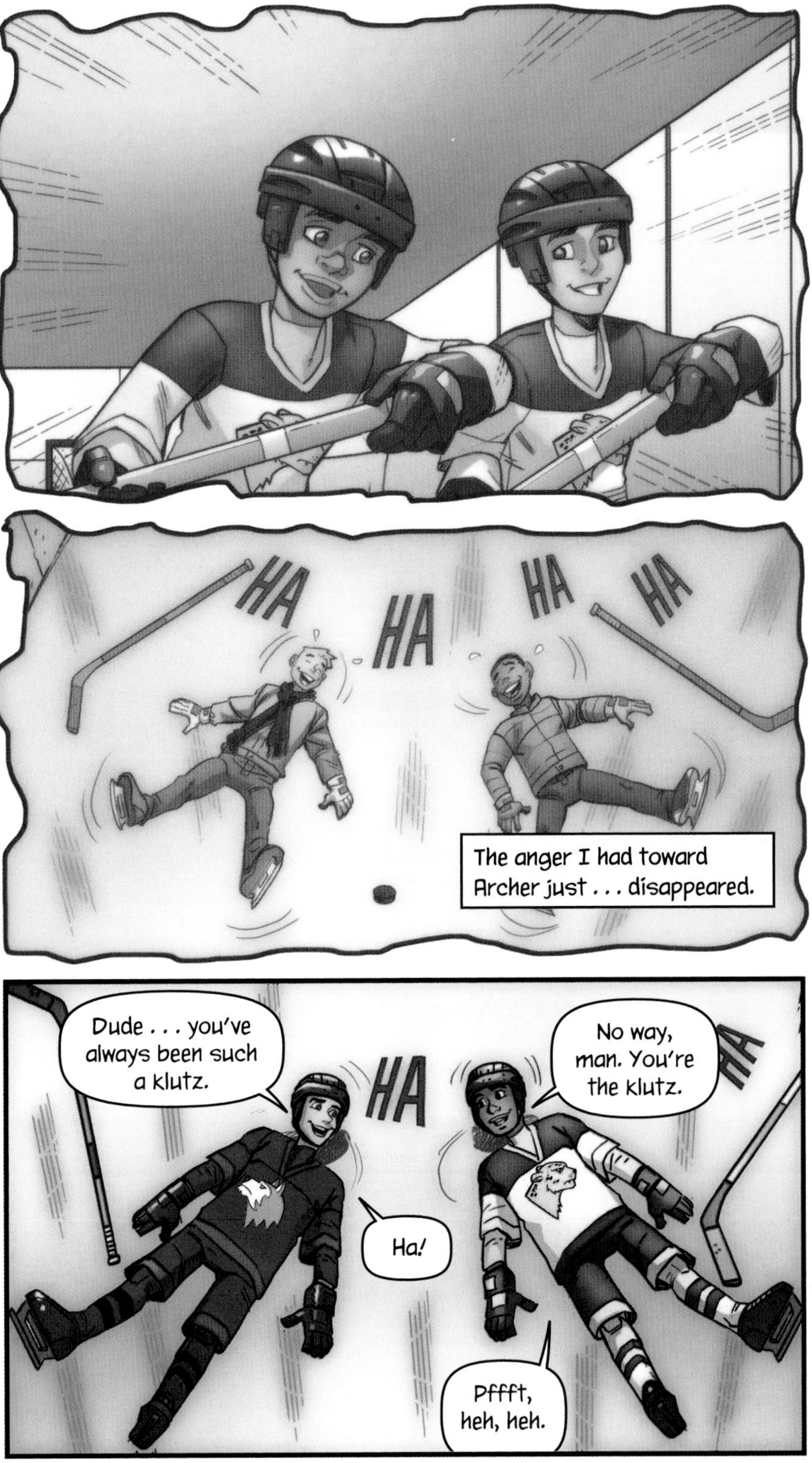
HA
HA
HA
HA
The anger I had toward Archer just . . . disappeared.
Dude . . . you've always been such a klutz.
HA
No way, man. You're the klutz.
HA
Ha!
Pffft, heh, heh.

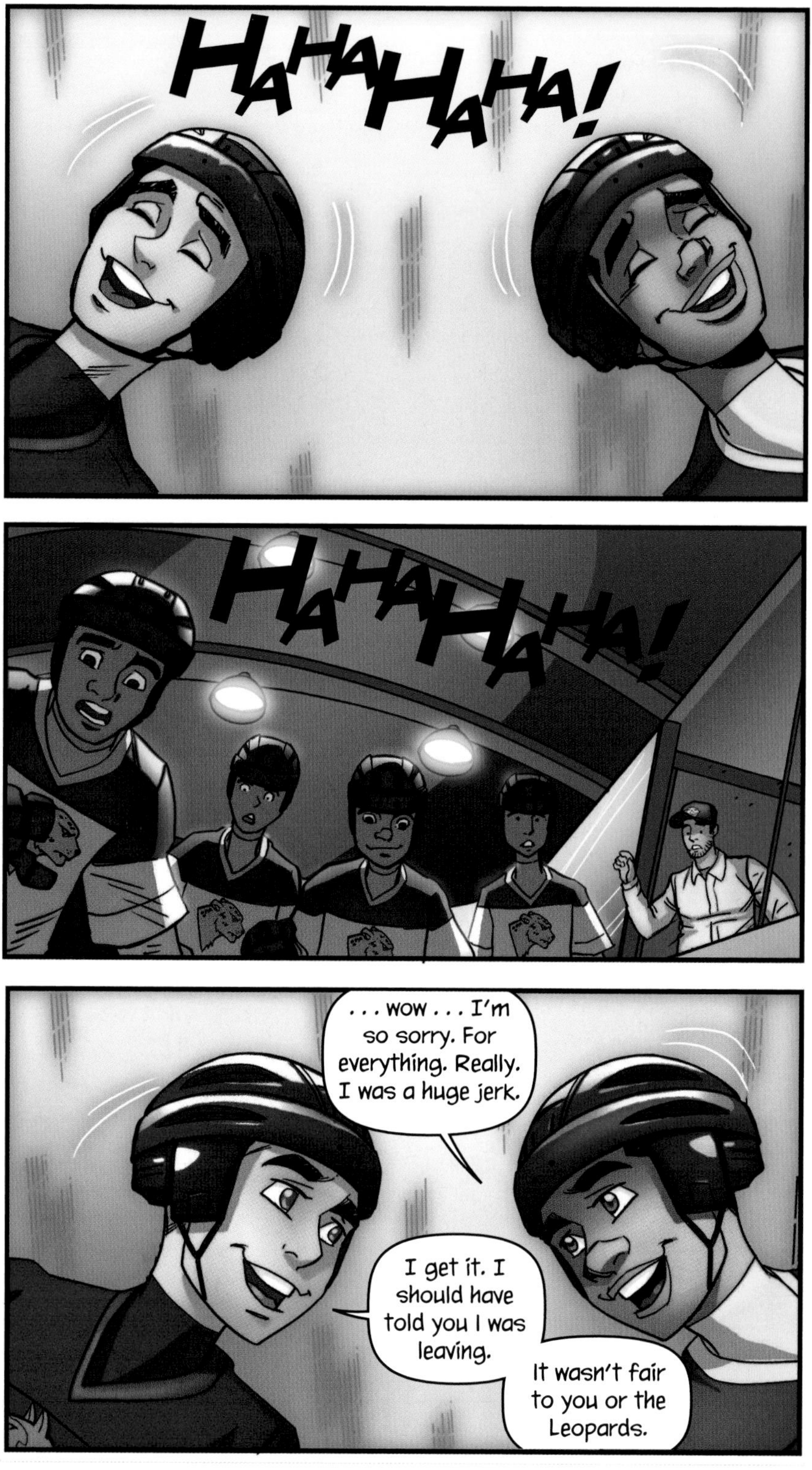
HAHAHAHAHAHA!
HAHAHAHAHAHA!
. . . wow . . . I'm so sorry. For everything. Really. I was a huge jerk.
I get it. I should have told you I was leaving.
It wasn't fair to you or the Leopards.

Well, yeah. But I should have been happy for you.

Instead I was only thinking about how losing you would affect me.

Um, you know there's a whole bunch of people watching us, right? We're kind of in the middle of an important game.

Yeah, we should probably chat later.

Over a Monster Grub Value Meal?

You know it!

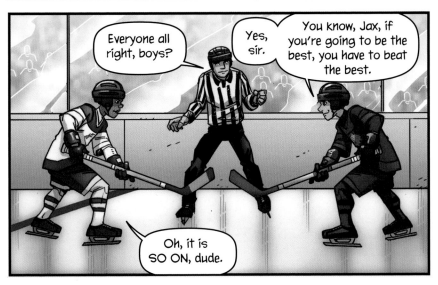

Everyone all right, boys?

Yes, sir.

You know, Jax, if you're going to be the best, you have to beat the best.

Oh, it is SO ON, dude.

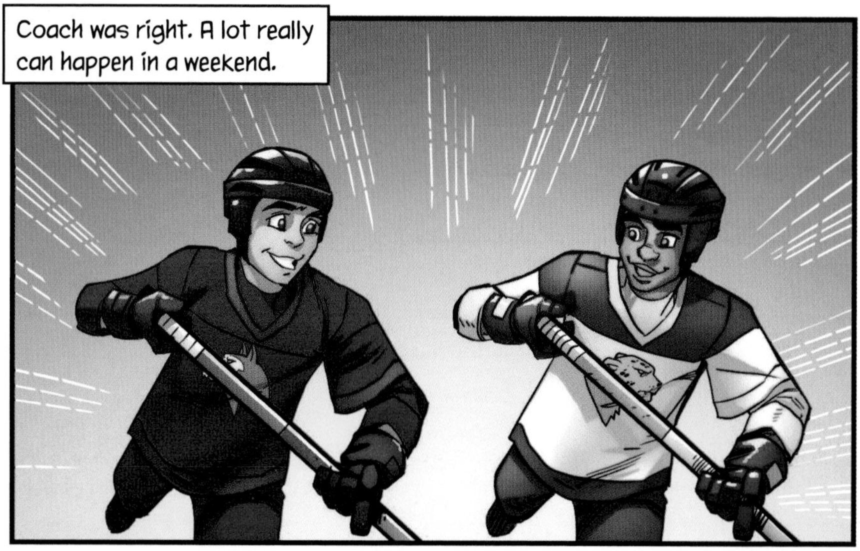
Coach was right. A lot really can happen in a weekend.

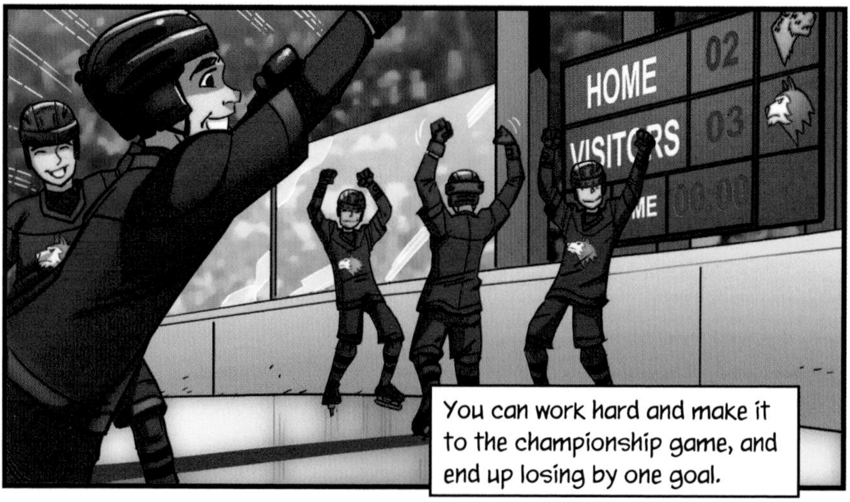
HOME
02
03
You can work hard and make it to the championship game, and end up losing by one goal.

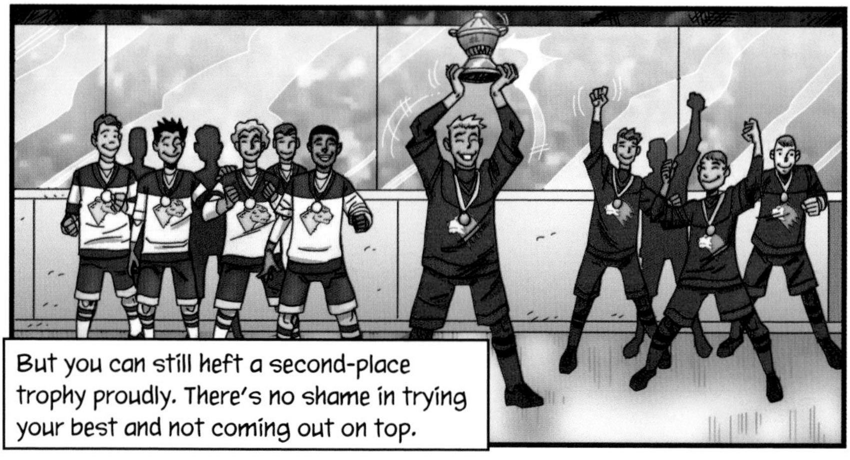
But you can still heft a second-place trophy proudly. There's no shame in trying your best and not coming out on top.

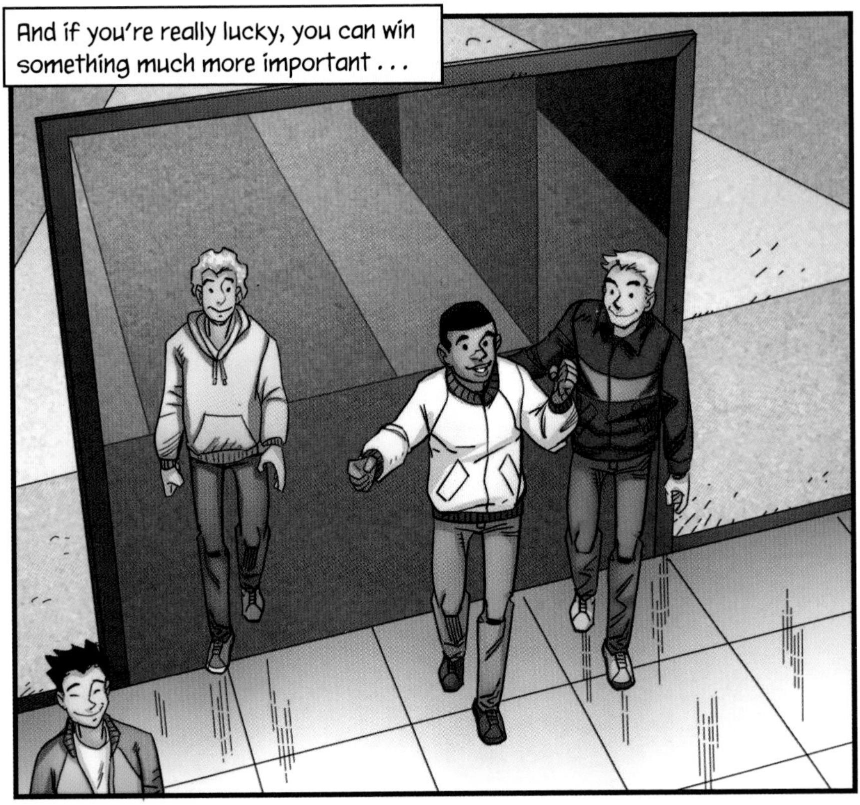
And if you're really lucky, you can win something much more important . . .

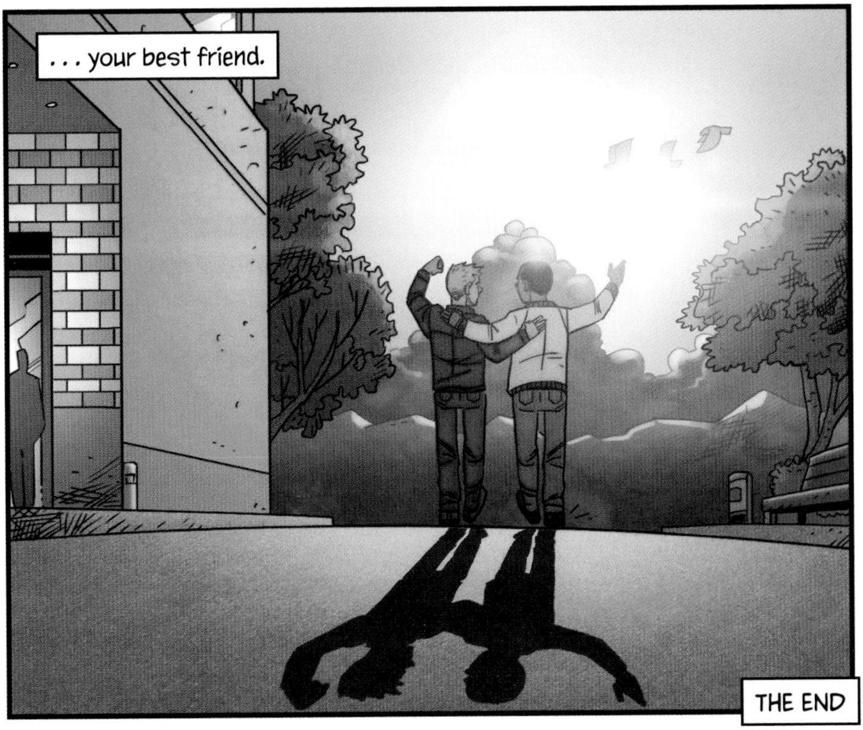
. . . your best friend.
THE END

VISUAL QUESTIONS

1. Flashbacks are often used to tell us about characters and what's happened in the past. What do we learn about Jax and Archer from the flashback panels seen here?

2. Graphic artists sometimes use a sequence of mirrored panels to help tell a story. What can we learn about the main characters from these mirrored panels?

  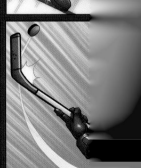

3. Study the panels to the right. What actions are being shown? Explain how these panels work together to show how Jax is feeling at this point in the story.

4. Facial expressions are important for showing us what a character is feeling at different parts of a story. Look at the panel below. What do you think Jax is feeling at this particular moment?

MORE ABOUT
ICE HOCKEY

- The origins of ice hockey are not completely known. Some people think it may have developed from stick and ball games played in Europe during the 1700s. When immigrants came to North America, they started playing the games on the ice during the winter. Eventually the games evolved into ice hockey.

- The first modern indoor ice hockey game was played in Montreal, Canada, in 1875.

- The National Hockey League (NHL) was founded on November 26, 1917, in Montreal, Canada. The first four teams in the league were all based in Canada. The first U.S. team, the Boston Bruins, joined the league in 1924.

- Frank Zamboni invented the first ice-clearing vehicle in 1949. Many similar devices have been invented since then. But today we still call the machine the Zamboni.

PENALTIES

If players break the rules, the referee calls a penalty. A penalty often results in the player spending time in the penalty box. Some common penalties include:

High-sticking — carrying the stick above the shoulders or when the stick makes contact above the shoulders of an opponent

Roughing — shoving another player after the whistle has blown or away from the play

Slashing — swinging the stick at an opponent

Tripping — using the stick, arm, or leg to trip an opponent

HOCKEY WORDS TO KNOW

CENTER — the player at the center forward position; centers are strong skaters and good at doing face-offs and getting the puck to the wingmen

CHECK — a move made with one's body or stick to stop an opponent's progress

DEFENSEMEN — two players on a hockey team who try to stop opposing players from taking shots on the team's goal

FACE-OFF — when the referee drops the puck between one player from each team; the players battle for possession of the puck to start or restart play

FORWARD — a player who has an attacking position and tries to score goals

GOALTENDER — the player who blocks opponents' shots and tries to keep the puck out of the net

POWER PLAY — when a team has a one- or two-player advantage because the other team has players in the penalty box

REFEREE — a person who supervises a sports match or game and enforces the rules

SLAP SHOT — the fastest and most powerful shot in hockey; a player raises the stick and slaps the puck hard toward the goal, putting his or her full power into the shot

WINGS — the two players at the left and right forward positions; wingmen are physical players who play mostly along the boards and in the corners

GLOSSARY

breakaway (BRAY-kuh-way)—a play in which an offensive player breaks free of the defenders and rushes toward the goal

championship (CHAM-pee-uhn-ship)—a final game in which the winning team is declared the league champion

distraction (dis-TRAK-shuhn)—something that causes someone to lose focus while performing a task

exhaustion (ek-ZAWS-chuhn)—the state of being extremely tired or of having no energy

goal (GOHL)—a point scored; also the netted area into which a puck must enter for a goal to be scored

overconfident (oh-vur-KON-fi-duhnt)—to have too much belief and trust in one's own abilities

overtime (OH-vur-time)—an extra period played if the score is tied at the end of a game

penalty (PEN-uhl-tee)—a punishment for breaking the rules of a game; the player has to sit in the penalty box for two or more minutes

period (PEER-ee-uhd)—an equal portion of playing time for an athletic game; hockey periods last 20 minutes

rhythm (RITH-uhm)—a regular pattern of movements, actions, and counteractions during a sporting event

ricochet (RIK-uh-shay)—when an object hits a hard surface and travels in a different direction

traitor (TRAY-tur)—someone who betrays the trust of others

READ THEM ALL!

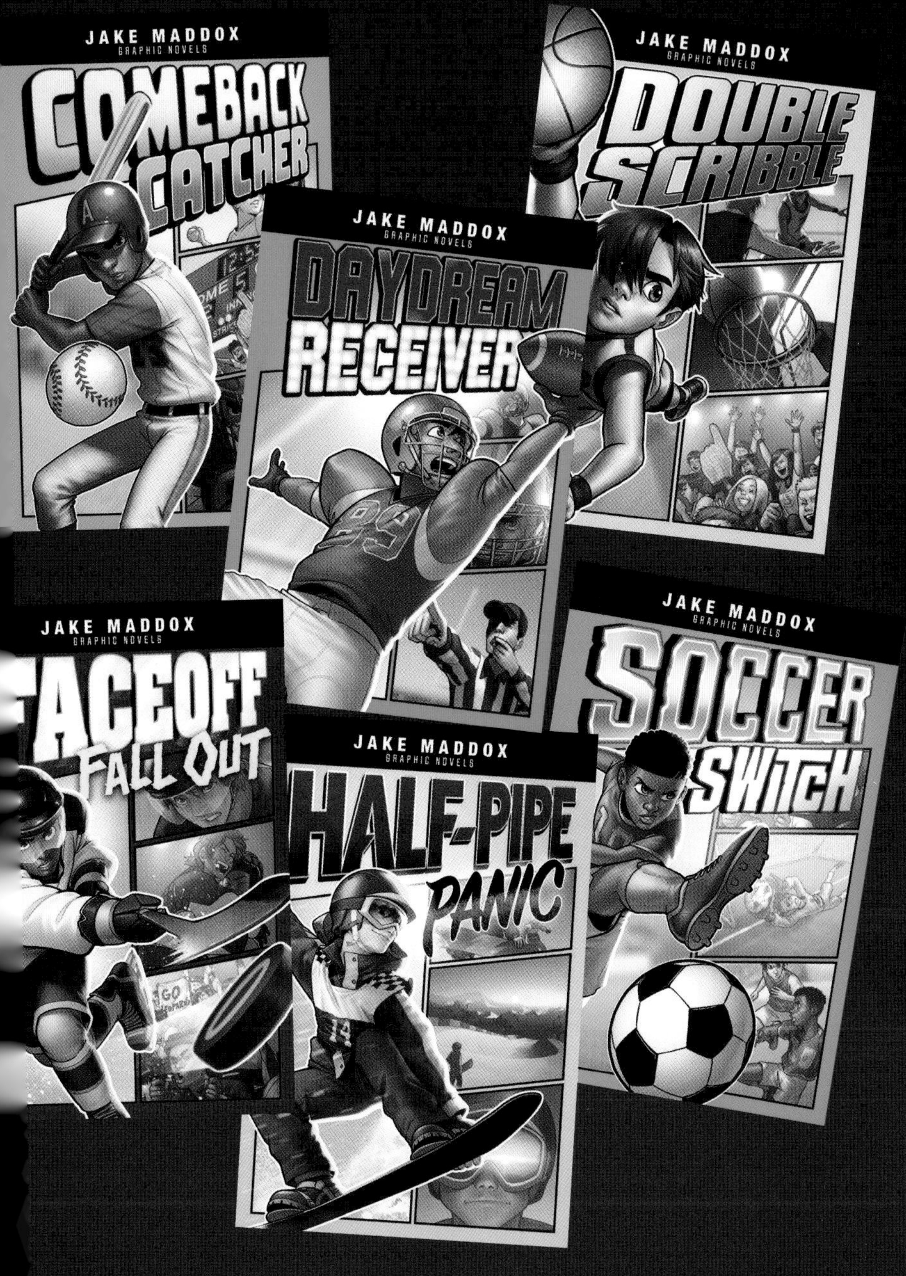
JAKE MADDOX GRAPHIC NOVELS
COMEBACK CATCHER
JAKE MADDOX GRAPHIC NOVELS
DOUBLE SCRIBBLE
JAKE MADDOX GRAPHIC NOVELS
DAYDREAM RECEIVER
JAKE MADDOX GRAPHIC NOVELS
FACEOFF FALL OUT
JAKE MADDOX GRAPHIC NOVELS
SOCCER SWITCH
JAKE MADDOX GRAPHIC NOVELS
HALF-PIPE PANIC

FIND OUT MORE AT
WWW.MYCAPSTONE.COM

ABOUT THE AUTHOR

Brandon Terrell is the author of numerous children's books, including several volumes in both the Tony Hawk 900 Revolution series and the Tony Hawk Live2Skate series. He has also written several Spine Shivers titles and is the author of the Sports Illustrated Kids: Time Machine Magazine series. When not hunched over his laptop, Brandon enjoys watching movies and TV, reading, watching and playing baseball, and spending time with his wife and two children at his home in Minnesota.

ABOUT THE ARTISTS

Eduardo Garcia works out of Mexico City. He has lent his illustration talents to such varied projects as the Spider-Man Family, Flash Gordon, and Speed Racer. He's currently working on a series of illustrations for an educational publisher while his wife and children look over his shoulder!

Benny Fuentes is a Mexican-based digital illustrator who has worked on several books,for companies such as Marvel, DC, Image Comics, and of course, Capstone Publishers. He also works as a volunteer at a local animal shelter during his free time.

Jaymes Reed has operated the company Digital-CAPS: Comic Book Lettering since 2003. He has done lettering for many publishers, most notably and recently Avatar Press. He's also the only letterer working with Inception Strategies, an Aboriginal-Australian publisher that develops social comics with public service messages for the Australian government. Jaymes is also a 2012 and 2013 Shel Dorf Award Nominee.